D0892896

Street of
Tall People

*My thanks to Bill Fishman,
Monty Richardson and
Harold Rosen*

Street of Tall People

by Alan Gibbons

Five Leaves Publications

www.fiveleaves.co.uk

Street of Tall People
by Alan Gibbons

Published in 2011
by Five Leaves Publications
PO Box 8786, Nottingham NG1 9AW
www.fiveleaves.co.uk

Street of Tall People was first published by Orion
This edition published by arrangement
with The Orion Publishing Group Limited, London.

ISBN: 978-1907869 23 5

Five Leaves acknowledges
financial support from
Arts Council England

Street of Tall People
is one of five books
published in celebration of
the Battle of Cable Street, 1936,
with the support of
the Barry Amiel and
Norman Melburn Trust

Design and typeset by
Four Sheets Design and Print

Printed in Great Britain

One

East End of London, 1936

He was afraid.

"Shake hands, boys."

Afraid. Jimmy Priest was afraid.

"Box!"

He eyed his opponent, a short, dark-haired boy crouching behind a high guard. For the first time in so many fights, it didn't seem to make sense. What were they doing here, facing up to each other like a pair of fighting cocks? There was a veil between them, a shifting membrane like the surface of dark waters, and Jimmy was sinking, engulfed by his fear.

"Come on, Jimmy; get into him!"

A boy's voice reached him shrilly from ringside. Jimmy took in his surroundings at a glance. The white emulsion paint on the walls of the club was flaking and there was damp mould in one corner. A picture of the new King hung askew to the right of the door — 'His Majesty, King Edward VIII.' The voices of the watching boys echoed dully as Jimmy's opponent abandoned his defensive stance and threw a couple of left handers.

"That's it, Benjamin! Good punches. Keep them like that, crisp and accurate."

Jimmy slid away from Benjamin's gloves and breathed deeply. It wasn't the dark, stocky boy he feared. He'd fought tougher kids, but there were worse things than the fists of this Benjamin, much worse.

His mind fastened on a day he would never forget, the day ten months before when things fell apart, the day he had learned to fear the world. He had walked into the sitting room clutching his presents, a paintbox and an orange, his cheeks stung by the frosty air and the thrill of the Christmas party.

"What's wrong?" he had asked, seeing the tears in his mother's eyes, the neighbours clustered grim-faced around her.

Then, like a distant roll of thunder, he heard shouts and was dimly aware of the boys around the ringside, drawing him back to the present, dispersing his memories. Jimmy saw Mr Devlin shaking his head as Benjamin began to open up. Encouraged by Jimmy's lack of fight, he had started slinging punches from all angles. Jimmy the fighter marvelled at his cheek, Jimmy the child flinched at the hurt flooding through him, overpowering him.

"Why's my mother crying?" he had asked, beginning to cross the living room. He'd wanted her to hold him, to stop crying, but hands had led him away.

"Come with me, Jim," Mrs Evans had whispered. "Leave your mum alone."

He had resisted. Why should he leave her? What had happened?

"I won't!" His voice was thin and anxious. "What's wrong with my mum?"

Then, in the tiny scullery his own tears had come. "What's happened?"

"It's your dad," Mrs Evans had told him. "He won't be coming home any more."

Jimmy remembered the fear rising in him, the clatter of the paintbox as he let it fall on the tiled floor, the gleam of the lid as it burst open.

Then the pain came — not the memory of it, but a real human fist. It crashed through his senses. Benjamin had caught him with a hook to the jaw.

"You've got him, Benny!" shouted a tall, powerfully-built boy. He was beating his fists excitedly on the bench where he sat with the other members of his club.

Jimmy's senses swam as Benny closed, jabbing hard into his stomach and chest. He clasped the pain to him, clinging to it.

"For goodness sake, Jimmy," shrieked the boys from his club, "fight back."

Jimmy didn't care what they called. They weren't his friends, just boys who turned up at the club. There had been a time when the club had mattered, but that was when his dad had brought him. Then he had understood what it was all about: pride in your own district, pride in yourself, growing to manhood through sport and companionship. But now? What was it for now?

"Fight back, Jimmy!"

This second time the words jerked him alive. Fight back. That was it. It was the only thing to do, not for the club or for anyone, just to strike back at the hurt and the fear. For a moment he saw the broken paintbox and the orange rolling forlornly into a corner of the scullery. 'Your dad's dead.' Then there was only the face, the smooth, olive face of a boy called Benny, and the need to fight back.

Jimmy came forward punching away to head and body, his long arms pumping in a series of frenzied attacks. He saw the look of surprise in Benny's eyes and he felt a deep satisfaction. He was pummelling the shorter boy's ribs and barely encountering any resistance. Jimmy was in a tunnel. It echoed with

Mrs Evans' voice as she told him his father was dead, and at the end of the tunnel was Benny's surprised, pained face. Jimmy was doing the only thing he was really good at. He was at war.

"Break."

Jimmy half turned at the voice. He was out of the tunnel, coming back.

"Break! Come on boys, the bell's gone."

Mr Devlin's voice guided him to his corner. "Look at me, Jim. Look up at me." The coach's dry, calloused hands were on his cheeks.

"You're crying."

"Mr Devlin. My dad..."

"I know Jimmy; he died."

Ten months before. They had told him on his return from the party at the church hall. It was Boxing Day afternoon.

"Try to think about something else," said Mr Devlin. "Once you started boxing you were backing him off."

The bell. Round two.

Mr Devlin gave Jimmy's cheeks a gentle pinch. "Just keep your mind on the bout. Use your strength and concentrate."

Jimmy took the centre of the ring and smacked his gloves into Benny's raised forearms. He knew nothing about this boy except that his name and the club to which he belonged made him Jewish.

"The Jews," the lads had told him, "they don't fight. We'll walk it."

Benny was crouching, bobbing his head left and right behind his raised arms.

"Go on Jim!" yelled the others.

Jimmy was gulping down mouthfuls of air, snatching at each breath as if it were his last.

8

Opposite him, Benny was now crouching so low it was barely possible to land a fair punch. Jimmy's next one, a savage uppercut, straightened him. Jimmy saw the same look of surprise cross Benny's features and pressed home his advantage, his long arms swinging. It was his only way out of the fear: fight, fight, fight.

"Jimmy's killing him!"

Then Mr Devlin's whispered admonishment, "He isn't scoring. He's got to direct his punches. Jimmy!" He shouted. "Jab! You're tiring yourself out."

But Jimmy was in the tunnel and in front of him was Benny's raised face. He was punching away to head and body but he was only hitting Benny's arms. As he sucked in another lungful of air he felt the effort scalding in his chest. His arms were tired, so tired.

"Keep your guard up!"

The warning came too late. As Jimmy's shoulders sagged, Benny shot out a hook. There was a warm, sticky taste in Jimmy's mouth. Blood. The bell rang and he followed Mr Devlin's voice to the corner.

"You're wearing yourself out swinging at him like that," said Mr Devlin. "You've got to think. Don't just fight, box."

Jimmy took a drink and spat into the towel.

"What is it, Jimmy?"

Jimmy grinned. "It's my tooth. He's knocked it out."

"I'll hang on to it for you," said Mr Devlin. "Now try to keep your head. Last round."

Jimmy nodded. At the bell he strode across the ring, meeting Benny with a couple of right-handers to the face.

For a split second Benny's eyes again registered surprise before he retreated behind his guard.

9

"Come on Benny; you're winning!"

Winning? Jimmy scowled. How could Benny be winning? Jimmy Priest wasn't the sort of boy to lose to a little runt like this.

But suddenly a punch to his stomach had Jimmy clinging to his opponent. He was panting and he was tired. He could hardly raise his arms. On the ref's instructions, Jimmy pushed Benny away but not before the smaller boy caught him with a left-hander as they broke.

"Jimmy!" cried the boys behind him. "Hit him back!"

But Jimmy was lost. The punches he'd taken in the first round had worn him down. The white-washed walls were spinning as he searched for Benny's face.

"Keep your guard up," Mr Devlin warned again.

Jimmy felt Benny's punches land, but they were at long last losing their sting. They were both tiring. While Benny pumped ineffective jabs at him, Jimmy could only throw out looping punches in the hope of landing one decent shot. It was no use.

"That's it, boys," announced the ref, shouting over the bell. "Well fought. The winner: Benny Silver."

Jimmy scowled. Defeat. The taste of it choked him. For ten months he had taken on anything life could throw at him. He had survived, but now he was losing. He couldn't go on. In his humiliation, he could see the man who had burst into his life only weeks before. Jimmy knew every detail of his face: the square jaw, the unblinking green eyes, the reddish-brown Brylcreemed hair and the pencil moustache. He detested that face, the face of a man who was stealing his life and burying his father a second time.

"I see your mother's got herself a new young man," Mrs Evans had said on the tenement stairs that morning. "It will do her good. It's no life for a woman on her own, not round here."

What did she know? His mother didn't need a new young man.

"Are you all right, boy?" asked Mr Devlin anxiously from the corner.

Jimmy nodded. He gave Benny a sideways glance. The boy was groggily accepting victory.

"Are you all right?" Mr Devlin repeated.

"I lost," said Jimmy. "And I feel like I'll never win again."

Two

"Did you see Benny fight?"

"A tiger we've got."

"He knocked the *kishkes* out of that big *yok*."

The final salute came from Yaro. And who else would it be? All the other boys in the club were as English as the Union Jack. That's how they saw themselves, a bunch of ordinary London boys growing up in their East End.

Unfortunately, not everyone saw it like that. There were people who turned resentful eyes on them. Yaro stood out. He'd heard the taunts of 'Jew boy' and he wanted to ram them down the throats which uttered them. He was a Jew first, second and last, and the only one who would readily tell you from which *shtetl* his family hailed. He was proud of his East European origins — fiercely proud — and that set him apart from the others. To them their ancestry was a fact, history, no more. To Yaro it was life itself.

"Your first fight and you walked it," said an admirer in the small crowd.

"I wouldn't say I walked it," said Benny as Yaro unlaced his gloves.

"And what would you say?" demanded Mr Jacobs.

"I don't know," Benny answered, stealing a glance at his dejected opponent. "I feel sorry for him."

"He was a good opponent," said Mr Jacobs. "One of their best."

"What was his name?" asked Benny. "Jimmy something."

"James Priest," said Mr Jacobs. "He has been boxing some time. I saw him when he boxed Oxford and St George's. He's a strong boy."

"Not strong enough," observed Yaro.

"*Oy!* Will you listen to yourself, Samuel?" groaned Mr Jacobs.

There were giggles. Nobody called Sam Yaroslavsky by his real name. He was Yaro to everyone. Even his parents had begun to take up the nickname.

"This boy," said Mr Jacobs, stabbing a finger at Jimmy Priest, "he reminds me of you, Samuel; big and strong and angry. You know why he's fighting? The world's hurt him, that's why. I can read it in his face, in the way he boxes. But if it's only anger he has, he will never make a boxer. One half of a boxer is made in here." He tapped his forehead. "You must use your strength and control your anger."

Yaro lowered his eyes like an ox being yoked. He resented Mr Jacobs' words, mainly because they were true.

"Now," said Mr Jacobs. "Get your gloves on. You're the last to box."

Benny watched as Mr Jacobs laced Yaro's gloves. Yaro sat silently, brooding over the rebuke. At fourteen he was two years older than Benny but he could easily pass for sixteen. He had powerful shoulders and fists like a man's. Benny smiled as he remembered what his *zaydeh* always said: 'With hands like that a presser he should be.'

Somehow Benny couldn't see Yaro working in the garment trade. The walls of a tailor's workshop just wouldn't contain him.

"Now," said Mr Jacobs. "Use your strength and leave your temper on the bench."

Another scowl from Yaro.

"Do you think he'll win, Mr Jacobs?" asked Benny.

"Win? He'll kill the boy."

"So why did he give Yaro such a hard time?" Benny whispered.

"Why do you think?" another boy replied. "He does it to give us an edge. Yaro's the only one who takes it seriously."

"Yaro takes everything seriously," said Benny.

Above them Yaro had his opponent trapped in a corner.

"He'll have a job to last the round out," said Mr Jacobs, nodding in the direction of Yaro's fair-haired victim as he sagged against the ropes. He was right. A few moments later the bout was stopped to save the boy from further punishment.

When Benny and Yaro emerged from the gloomy premises into the bright early autumn sunshine, Jimmy was waiting for them.

"Here," said Jimmy, holding out a sweet wrapper. "I've got something for you."

"What is it?" asked Benny suspiciously. Unlike Yaro he didn't think that if you scratched a *goy* you found a Jew-baiter, but he was cautious. He had read the conflicting emotions on Jimmy's face as he proffered the wrapper.

"Take a look."

Benny inspected the package, then smiled. "It was my first fight, you know."

Jimmy coloured. "Your first?"

"My mum was against it. Me too, if the truth be known, but my dad thought it was a good idea. He says you want to live in this country, you take part in everything they do. And if you take part, you make sure you're the best."

"And he was right," Yaro interrupted. "Give the *goyim* a taste of their own medicine."

Benny ignored Yaro's interruption. "I live in Whitechapel. Behind the hospital. And you?"

"Off Globe Road. Do you know Empire Mansions?"

Benny shook his head.

"I'd better go," said Jimmy. He'd taken a shine to Benny, but it was still hard to talk to his conqueror.

"Say," Benny called as Jimmy walked away. "Do you ever go to Victoria Park?"

"Of course. Why?"

"We'll be there this Sunday. We might see you there."

"Yes, maybe," said Jimmy.

"What made you say that?" asked Yaro. He was not happy. Not one bit.

"It just came into my head," Benny answered.

"That head," grumbled Yaro. "You should use it more."

"What do you mean?"

"You tell the *yok* where to find us and you don't think he'll be there with a gang of roughs?"

"Why should he be?"

Yaro snorted. This year of all years a good *Yiddishe* boy should ask that. Was there a soul in the Jewish East End who hadn't heard of Mosley's Blackshirts and their reign of terror?

"Yaro doesn't trust anybody who doesn't go to *shul*," observed one of the other boys.

"Yaro doesn't trust anybody, full stop," said Benny pointedly.

It was true. To this big bear of a boy there were two tribes in the East End: the Jews which was them and the *yoks* which was everybody else.

15

"Such nonsense you talk!" snapped Yaro.

They started walking in the direction of Whitechapel.

"There was something I wanted to ask you," said Yaro, pausing at the street corner.

"Then ask."

"What did he give you? Sweets?"

Benny lowered his eyes. He had hoped he wouldn't have to answer.

"Well?"

"See for yourself."

Yaro poked at the package with a thick, stubby forefinger. "A tooth? The *yok* gives you a tooth?"

"It's the one I knocked out," explained Benny. "I think it's a sort of memento, a trophy."

"You call that a trophy?" asked Yaro, examining the small white tooth.

Benny crumpled the wrapper. "You think it's stupid?"

Yaro shook his head. "I *know* it's stupid. He'll be hiding somewhere, laughing at you."

Benny felt the roughness of the sweet paper against his palm and thought of Jimmy. He felt that this was one *goy* who needed a friend, but how could he tell that to Yaro? Again he squeezed the wrapper. It was a small gesture, like a handshake. It recognised him as a man, a *mensch*.

"You're not going to keep it?" asked Yaro, disgusted.

Benny didn't want a row, not with Yaro who had been his friend and protector for more years than he could remember. Slowly, he shook his head and tossed the package into the gutter.

"No, I'm not going to keep it."

Three

"Here he is now. How are you doing, Jimmy boy?"

Jimmy avoided Mr Searle's eyes. When his dad was alive, there had always been grumbles about him. Nobody in the tenements had a good word for the rent collector. He was just the landlord's runner and the butt of their complaints. There was no shortage of them either. Empire Mansions was a cheerless block of cramped, dilapidated flats. The tenants had a lot to moan about: if it wasn't the damp, it was the faulty gas lights, the vermin, the lack of repairs. Now here was the same rent collector, a regular guest in the flat. Jimmy grimaced; he was certainly making himself at home.

Eddie Searle crossed his legs. He always stood out as he did his rounds. He was a natty dresser in his light grey sports jacket, well-pressed flannel trousers and open-necked shirt. Mrs Evans said he looked like a film star, a real Ronald Coleman or George Raft.

"So how did you do, old son?"

Jimmy shuddered. 'Old son!'

"I lost."

"Knocked you down, did he?"

"No, I stayed on my feet. I got angry, that's all. I didn't use my loaf."

"Now will you listen to the boy!" said Mr Searle with an approving smile. "He knows a bit about boxing, this boy of yours."

Jimmy's mother smiled. "More tea, Eddie?"

"No thanks, I'd better be off in a minute. Lots to do yet." Mr Searle tapped his notebook. "It's like

17

painting the Forth Bridge, this job of mine. The moment you come to the end of your round it's time to start all over again."

He laughed loudly as if he'd cracked a good joke.

"So which club were you boxing against today?"

The moment Jimmy mentioned the club's name, the smile vanished from Mr Searle's face. "Are you telling me you got beaten by some little Jewboy?" His anger surfaced suddenly, brutally, taking Jimmy unawares.

"Well, is that right?"

Jimmy nodded. He glimpsed his mother's face. She looked startled by the outburst.

Catching her eye, Eddie Searle's hawkish expression softened. "Did I frighten you then, Jimmy? I'm sorry, but where's your bulldog spirit? I don't like to see an English boy beaten by ... by one of *them.*"

One of them! Despite his defeat, Jimmy didn't really blame Benny. His real opponent was sitting in the chair opposite. Jimmy felt nervous.

"Do you want me to give you some lessons, Jim? I box at the Institute myself. I give some of the lads a bit of training."

"Would you like that, Jimmy?" his mother asked. She sounded eager for him to like Mr Searle.

"I don't know." He was flustered. It wouldn't be right. That was the sort of thing he'd always done with his dad.

"Mum," he said, desperate to escape, "is there anything to eat?" He could sense Searle watching him and his neck was prickling. Please, he thought, please leave me alone.

"You can have a round of bread and margarine," she said. "I've got some scrag end for your tea."

Jimmy retreated gratefully to the scullery and began to spread a film of margarine on his bread. He could hear the low tones of Mr Searle and his mother's laughter. It sounded strange, girlish, and Jimmy hated it.

"Well, I'll be off," said Mr Searle as he reached the front door. "I won't make my fortune chatting here. Tomorrow night then, Grace. About seven?"

"Yes," said Jimmy's mother. "Seven's fine. I'll look forward to it."

"Bye, Jimmy," said Mr Searle, poking his head round the scullery door. "And keep that guard up. Don't forget about those lessons. I'll soon give you a few pointers."

Jimmy smiled weakly and retreated behind the pantry door until he heard the front door close.

"Is he taking you out?" he asked.

"That's right," said his mother, unable to disguise her excitement. "We're going to see a film, then go for a few drinks. Maybe a bite to eat."

Jimmy dropped the bread knife into the sink.

"Is something wrong, Jim? You don't mind Mr Searle calling, do you?"

"No."

"Come on, get it off your chest."

"Are you going to marry him?"

His mother laughed, a loud forced laugh. "Oh, you are a silly boy!"

Jimmy could hear the voices of the kids playing on the staircases and in the streets below.

"I think I'll play out."

"Not before you talk to me."

Jimmy shifted his feet uneasily.

"Come and sit by me," said his mother.

Jimmy drew a chair up to the heavily scored

kitchen table. The chair leg scraped against the broken linoleum.

"You shouldn't worry," she reassured him. "It's nothing. Just a drink. A woman needs company."

"I'm company."

"And you're good company, of course you are. I couldn't want for a better son. I mean adult company."

"What about Mrs Evans?"

His mother reached across and took his hands. "Don't do this, Jimmy. You know what I mean. A man friend."

She examined his face as if searching for his blessing.

"What happened to your tooth?" she asked abruptly.

"It happened down at the club," Jimmy explained. "I was up against this lad called Benny." He paused, then leaned forward. "Mum."

"Yes?"

"I was thinking. Do you remember the way Mr Searle lost his temper with me for losing?"

His mother looked uncomfortable.

"Why did he do that? Doesn't he like Jews?"

"Maybe he does and maybe he doesn't. That's his business. I don't mind them, they never did me any harm, but not everybody thinks like I do." She began to get up.

"So you wouldn't mind if I made friends with Benny?"

"Do you know him that well?"

"I only met him today, but we might meet again."

"Where's he from?"

"Whitechapel. Somewhere behind the hospital."

"We don't go down there much," his mother said doubtfully.

"We have been," said Jimmy. "Don't you remember when you lost me near Brick Lane?"

"I certainly do," his mother answered, "but I didn't think you would. You must have only been four or five."

"I've never forgotten it," said Jimmy. "Suddenly I was all on my own. Everybody seemed so big; it was a street of tall people. I couldn't see anything for these big men. They were wearing long black coats and black hats and they had beards. They were rattling on in this foreign lingo. I was so scared I wanted to scream but I couldn't make the sound."

"Poor Jim," said his mother. "I know they look strange to us, but my family came from Ireland. We must have seemed strange once. And don't forget, it was one of those gentlemen that brought you back to me."

"I remember him leading me by the hand," said Jimmy. "I wanted to run and hide. I thought he was going to take me away. I couldn't get it out of my mind for days after."

His mother smiled and rested her hand on his shoulder.

"But why doesn't Mr Searle like them?"

"I don't know," she replied. "Maybe he's got his reasons."

Jimmy felt frustrated by her answer. What reasons? He found it hard to make sense of the day's events. The men in black coats were Jews, that tough little fighter Benny was also a Jew. Then Mr Searle had been angry because he'd lost to a Jew. Jimmy peered out of the window at the dusk gathering over the tenements. The first streetlamps were shining blearily in the street below, and in the twilight the mystery hung as heavy as overripe fruit.

Four

"You know, Benny," his *zaydeh* would say, "you have the dreams of a grammar school boy. You have the dreams of an educated man."

It hadn't made much sense at the time, especially when he had only just started at the grammar school. Now, like most of the pearls which fell from his grandfather's lips, it was beginning to. He couldn't help but see his present mission as a grand adventure.

Benny's head was stuffed with heroes and they all lived in the reading room at Whitechapel Library. Just then Benny needed his heroes. He was walking along streets a Jewish boy didn't walk alone, and for what? The tooth of a *goy* he hardly knew, wrapped in an old sweet paper.

"You know what Yaro would call you, Benny boy?" he whispered to himself. "A *narr* is what he would call you — a complete fool."

But isn't it also a fool who fails to take the hand of friendship?

"So what if I am?" murmured Benny. "Better a fool than a coward!"

Brave words for a twelve-year-old boy hurrying along the darkening streets of enemy territory. He knew the unwritten law: thus far and no further. Hadn't it been hammered home, especially in the last few months as the fascist attacks grew more frequent, as the newspaper columns filled with attacks on Jews and rallies of uniformed men. Cross that road and leave the safety of your own quarter and you're asking for trouble.

His mind filled with the stories he'd heard, darkly told by the little knots of grown-ups who gathered on the pavement until late in the evening to escape the bed bugs. He knew their tales by heart. He knew about the streets where they used to pull the beards of Jews. He knew about the men in black shirts who used fists and boots if you were lucky and coshes and knuckledusters if you weren't. He knew that armies of men like them had stormed to power in Europe and wanted to do the same here.

"Two more streets," Benny told himself, forcing such ideas to the back of his mind.

To banish the men in their black shirts he told himself a story of his own making. It was his best story: the story of the boy who always had his nose in a book, learns his lessons well and passes the scholarship to the grammar school. The story of a boy who makes his mother and father proud and who, one day, will be — who knows ? — a doctor or a lawyer. What did they say in the films? A big shot. Benny liked that — a big shot.

"This is it," he said aloud as he turned into the narrow street where the boys' club stood.

Would it still be there? One tiny scrap of paper in the dry, dusty gutter. "It is!"

He rushed forward eagerly, picked up the wrapper and checked the contents. There it was: a white tooth half worn away because it had stayed too long in the head of its owner, the same tooth he had knocked out in his very first fight.

He knew what was said about his people, of course. Hadn't his father told him often enough? The meek Jew. Jew-baiters pulled our fathers' beards and they just bowed their heads and hurried by.

"I wonder if you think *I'm* meek, Jimmy?" Benny

asked, a smile spreading across his lips. Triumphantly he turned back towards Spitalfields.

"Hey," came a voice. "What have we got here?"

"Looks like a Jew boy to me. Lost, are you?"

Benny's heart kicked. There were four of them — no, five.

"What brings you round here, *Hymie*?" came the mocking taunt. "Come to sell us a suit?"

Benny started to walk. He was in *shtook* this time.

"Is it something I said?" asked the tallest of the group, probably their ring-leader. His remark provoked loud laughter.

Benny took a deep breath. One of the group was standing a little apart from his friends. There was only one way to go, straight at him. Benny was aware of the tooth in its wrapper closed tightly in his fist. *His* tooth now, his trophy, his pride.

"*Volla, volla* Jewboy!" The mocking chant echoed loudly down the twilit street.

One way to go. He had to make his move, and quickly. He weighed up the boy who was barring his way.

"You're not so tough," he said under his breath.

The footsteps were coming closer. It was now or never. Without another moment's thought, Benny rushed forward and crashed his fist into the boy's chest. He marvelled at his own power. This tooth he had won in battle was like a magic talisman giving him superhuman strength. He smiled grimly when he heard the short, strangled moan: "Urrgh!"

"Get him!"

"A coward's trick. He hit Johnny without so much as a warning."

"Coward's trick! Coward's trick!"

"Cut him off."

Cut him off at the pass! That's what it said in the cowboy stories. "Not this Indian," panted Benny as he pounded round the corner. Not this Indian.

The gang were running hard, two behind him, three on the opposite side of the road, ready to block his escape. There were no taunts now. Benny was a good runner, and they had no spare breath to waste on insults. He wasn't just fast either; he had stamina. One on one he would have beaten any of them, but their numbers gave them an advantage. Sooner or later they were bound to outflank him. Glancing behind he noted that his pursuers were down to four. Maybe he would make it after all. Still clutching the tooth Benny turned the last corner which would lead him back onto home territory.

"Thought you'd got away, didn't you?" Benny's heart turned over. It was the fifth member of the gang. Somehow he'd found a short cut.

Benny skidded to a halt and looked around.

"Forget it," said the boy facing him. "You're not going anywhere."

Benny was aware of the group behind him. They had slowed to a walk. He took a deep breath and waited for the first blow.

"Get him!"

The roar, then running feet. Benny felt a kick in his calf, then fingers pressing his eyes. A red mist clouded his vision. Unable to see, he began to lash out with his fists.

"Pin his arms."

He was struggling violently as two pairs of hands gripped him.

"Get him to the ground!" came the breathless command of the gang leader.

The words were like a prong in Benny's side. It was Yaro's golden rule: whatever you do, stay on your feet. If they get you on the ground you've had it.

"Stay on your feet, Benny boy," he told himself.

"Ow!" The cry gave Benny hope. His swinging fists had found their mark.

"Get hold of the little blighter!"

"I'll knock his block off for that," snarled the boy Benny had caught.

"You think so, do you?"

Benny jerked his head round at the new voice, glimpsing a familiar face between his attackers' fingers. Yaro!

"Push off," one of Benny's tormentors said. "This is none of your business."

Yaro wrinkled his nose with distaste. Who were they to tell him his business?

Sensing his chance, Benny dug his elbow into the stomach of the boy to his right and rushed towards Yaro.

"We're not scared of you," announced the tallest of them. "It's five onto two."

Yaro didn't answer. He was standing with his feet planted apart, his brawny arms tensed at his sides.

"Go on then," said the leader, sauntering up to him. "Want to make something of it?"

Yaro turned his brown eyes on the boy, then cuffed him aside. The slap looked almost casual, but Benny knew that it had hurt.

"Well, don't just stand there!" The gang leader was nursing his jaw. "There's more of us than them."

His friends were shifting their feet. Their courage was draining away.

"Five onto two. What's up with you?"

That's when Yaro's patience finally wore thin. Reaching into his pocket, he drew something out.

"He's got a club."

Yaro had started using the weapon the summer before. He had been chased by some street roughs. Yaro had vowed never to run again. Ever since, he'd been carrying a piece of an old chair leg round with him. Just in case.

"Run for it!"

Benny turned to Yaro. "Thanks."

"You want to thank me?" snapped Yaro, as they headed for Gardiner's Corner and safety. "Stay in your own streets, that's how to thank me."

Benny nodded, though of course, he had no intention of following Yaro's advice. A boy who dreams of sunsets on the snows of Kilimanjaro and cloudbursts over the Amazon will never be satisfied with a few narrow streets in the East End. They had reached Woolworth's, the big store with its familiar red-on-gold facade which dwarfed Goldenfeld's and Specter's next door. A few minutes' walk further on were their own streets with their synagogues, tailors' shops and bakeries and the sooty air which rang with crisp Yiddish phrases.

"I don't understand you," said Yaro, tapping Benny's hand. "For this you nearly get your ribs kicked in? All that *schlemozzel* for a tooth?"

Benny's eyes widened. "You know why I went?"

"Of course I know. Maybe that *yok* at the boys' club hit you harder than I thought. He must have scrambled your brains."

Benny didn't even try to argue with Yaro. What was the point?

"Well?" demanded Yaro gruffly. "Was it worth the trouble?"

"I think so," said Benny. How could he say otherwise? "Yes, I'm sure it was."

Five

"I see your mum's found a way to get her rent lowered."

The words were Tubby Morrissey's.

"What?"

"Your old lady and her rent collector? Very cosy." Tubby gave a knowing wink.

"Take that back!" yelled Jimmy. He was hot with humiliation and rage. Was his mother's new chap common knowledge already?

The eyes of every boy and girl in the block were on Jimmy's flushed, angry face. Tubby's taunt had echoed round the drab walls of the tenements, some of them still hung with bunting from Coronation Day. The other children knew him for a fighter, always a fighter, but Tubby was thirteen and built like a brick wall.

Tubby too was aware of an audience slowly drifting in their direction. He reached out for the rope tied to one of the lamp-posts and began to tug on it. "Still, it's one way to get by on a widow's pension."

"Stop it!" said Jimmy. "Just stop saying that or ..."

"Or what?"

"Or I'll make you eat your words."

Tubby gave a long, low whistle. "My, my, you are touchy, aren't you?"

A girl in a faded green dress giggled. Jimmy wanted the earth to eat him up.

"So when's the big day?" Tubby continued, still playing with the rope. "When does your mum become Mrs Searle?"

He started to hum the wedding march. "Dum dum da dum, dum dum da dum, dum dum da da da..."

"I told you to stop," cried Jimmy, tears stinging his eyes. He glanced up the tenements to his flat where even now his mother was getting ready to go up West with Eddie Searle.

Tubby was warming to his theme. "Altogether now."

Soon Jimmy found himself standing in the middle of a circle of children, each of them chanting that stupid wedding march.

"Stop it!"

Jimmy tried to push his way out of the circle but the group had linked arms and threw him back.

"Stop!"

"Anything wrong?"

Jimmy spun round to face Eddie Searle. His heart thudded in his chest. If there was anybody he didn't want to see, it was him.

"This lot bothering you, Jim?"

Jimmy shook his head miserably.

"I'll see you after, then."

For a few moments as Mr Searle strode across the road everything stopped. He cut a dashing figure. Tall and broad-shouldered, he looked every bit the all round sportsman Jimmy had been told about.

"That suit cost a bob or two, I'll bet," said Tubby, breaking the silence.

"You're in the money, young Priest."

"I told you to stop that," said Jimmy.

"What, when I'm having so much fun?"

"I'll kill you!"

Jimmy was standing with his fists clenched, his whole body shaking. His eyes were blazing with rage.

"Just look at him," said Tubby, playing to his

audience. "I think he's got a problem."

There was fire in Jimmy's soul. Deep inside him there had been so many seeds of this great anger: the pain of loss, the cold gnaw of loneliness, the bitter resentment at Searle's intrusion in his life. Now each was germinating into a sturdy growth and its name was fury.

"Anyway, good luck to you, Jimmy. You'll never go without if you've got a rent collector for a dad."

Jimmy's rage boiled over. He flew at Tubby.

"Jimmy!"

He stopped dead in front of the older boy, halted by his mother's cry.

"Jimmy. Come up here this minute."

He looked into Tubby's smirking face.

"Go on, Jimmy," said Tubby, still grinning. "Run on home to Mummy."

The anger had gone. All that was left was shame. As Jimmy made his way to the tenement stairs the wedding march resumed behind him. "Dum dum da dum..."

His mother met him at the top of the stairs. "What was all that about? Were you fighting again?"

"I wasn't fighting."

"It looked that way to me."

Jimmy dug his hands deep in his pocket and looked past his mother at Mr Searle.

"Were they making fun of you?" she asked. "What about?"

Jimmy brushed past. "It doesn't matter."

The burning sensation spread across his shoulder. The bed bugs were biting again. He remembered what Mrs Evans had said before she sent him to bed: "I hope you get some sleep. The Red Army's on the march tonight."

Jimmy hated the bugs. Sometimes he and his mother went on a bug hunt, picking the eggs, but they always came back.

"Couldn't sleep anyway," Jimmy grumbled, sitting up in bed.

He stared at the cracked ceiling and the peeling wallpaper and listened to the voices drifting up from the street. He strained for his mother's but he couldn't hear her.

"You still awake, Jim?" called Mrs Evans.

"Yes," he answered. "It's the bed bugs."

"Come and sit with me then," she said.

Gratefully Jimmy walked into the sitting room, padding over the threadbare mat in his bare feet.

"Do you think she'll marry him?" Jimmy asked.

"A bit previous, aren't you Jimmy?" chuckled Mrs Evans. "It's the first time he's taken her out."

Jimmy stared across at his parents' wedding photograph, his father in a brown suit and his mother in a white dress, stockings, shoes and cloche hat.

"Thinking about your dad?"

Jimmy nodded.

"He was a good fellow, your dad; thoughtful."

"So why's she forgetting all about him?"

"Forget her Harry? Not your mother. She's lonely, that's all."

"How can she be lonely? She's got me."

Mrs Evans smiled. "You're too young to understand."

But he wasn't. He knew exactly what was going on. His world, the fragile world he had so carefully put together after his father's death, was coming to an end.

"Hello," said Mrs Evans. "That sounds like them

33

now."

Sure enough, Mr Searle opened the door for his mother and guided her in by the arm. Her cheeks were flushed. A tremor went through Jimmy; this man made her happy.

"Oh Jimmy," grumbled his mother, "what are you doing up?"

"Don't blame the boy," said Mrs Evans, springing to his defence. "It was the bugs. Eating him alive, they were."

He saw his mother give Mr Searle a little sideways glance.

"Well ladies," he said cheerfully, "I'd better be off."

He bent forward to say goodnight to Jimmy. His breath smelt of beer and tobacco. "Take care of your mother for me," he said.

Take care of her *for you*! Jimmy clenched his fists until his nails dug white crescents into the flesh of his palm. He watched Searle striding to the door, detesting him and his jaunty parting.

"Goodnight, all!"

Six

"Let's go to the lake first," said Yaro.

They raced down the tree-lined path and over the wooden bridge.

"There's the Pagoda!" shouted Benny. He loved the large, ornate Chinese pagoda with its red roof and green walls. It was special, like seeing a unicorn in a wooded glade. Who would have thought of such an idea? A pagoda in East London! It was a dream.

"Shall we get a rowing boat?" Yaro suggested.

"Too dear," said Benny. "Let's save some of our money for the motor launch."

"I'd rather have a rowing boat," Yaro said hopefully.

"Maybe later," said Benny.

Yaro muttered something under his breath but he yielded easily. Big and strong as he was, he always gave way. Benny was the guiding light of their odd partnership, if not the brains, then at least the inspiration.

"Not much of a queue today, is there?" said Benny.

"No, we'll get on first go," said Yaro. As they joined a line of chattering, pushing boys and girls there was a great cheer. The launch chugged into sight round the island at the centre of the park lake. The moment it stopped everybody swarmed past the bemused boatman and started jostling for the best places.

"Now give over shoving," he said. "Don't your parents tell you how to behave?"

He might well have saved his breath. The moment the propeller started churning everybody was hanging over the edge, trailing their hands in the water. There was a lot of shouting and screaming and they were off, pulling steadily away from the bank.

"Hey, Yaro," said Benny as they skirted the island. "Isn't that Jimmy?" He was pointing through a waterfall known as 'the cataract'. The play of the sun through the spray of falling water created a rainbow and through it he could see Jimmy waving.

"See," said Benny, "he never brought any toughs along with him. I told you he was all right."

Yaro snorted.

When the launch pulled back into the bank at the end of the ride Jimmy was waiting.

"You came then," said Benny.

"It looks like it," said Jimmy.

"Where are your pals?"

Jimmy looked puzzled.

"The boys from your club."

"They're not my pals," said Jimmy. "I just box with them."

Benny wondered what to make of this blunt reply, but after a moment or two he decided to let it pass.

"Are we going rowing?" asked Yaro.

"I haven't got any money," said Jimmy.

"A walk then," said Benny.

"A walk?" grumbled Yaro. "Walking's for your *zaydeh*. I say we go rowing."

"I'd rather walk," said Jimmy.

"It looks like you're outnumbered," said Benny.

"Why do we have to do what the *yok* wants?" demanded Yaro.

"*Yok*, Jew — what does it matter?" Benny replied testily, as they crossed Grove Road to the fields. "I just want to be me, Benny Silver, man of the world, explorer, star of the silver screen."

"You talk stupid," said Yaro. "You can't change what you are."

"And why not? Who says?" He smiled at Yaro's knotted brows. It was just like him. Oh, his big bear of a friend had dreams, but they were hewn out of the brick and tarmac of Whitechapel. As for Benny, his mind flew far and wide beyond the bounds of the East End. He wanted to see a flying boat bump on to the waters of an Asian river; he wanted to see the sunset on the Nile; he wanted to feel the snows of Kilimanjaro on his face and hear the crash of thunder over a lost world.

As they walked back to the park they passed the forum. The open space was filled with soapbox speakers.

"Boring," said Yaro. He was still sulking about the rowing boat.

But Benny and Jimmy had stopped by a speaker in a shabby blue serge suit and a greasy cap. He was thin and his baggy trousers flapped ridiculously around his long legs.

"You may laugh," said the speaker, answering a heckler, "but what I'm saying is right. There's a reign of terror going on in our East End. Every time they spout their hatred, every time they get away with beating somebody up, they're closer to their aim. Some day soon they'll try to claim this area for their own. They'll march, and if we don't stop them they'll have us by the throat. Mosley's fascists are trying to do here what Hitler's stormtroopers did in Germany."

He was cut off by a mocking jeer of "Up the revolution!"

"Right," the speaker countered. "You know I won't

argue with that."

A loud groan from a woman in a flowered dress standing next to the boys.

"But what I'm telling you is true. Over there the Jews have been beaten and thrown out of their jobs, and now it's happening here too. The day of reckoning's coming."

This was met by shouts of "Go back to Russia!" More hecklers were joining in and the speaker started to trade insults with a red-faced man on the far side of the crowd.

"Come on," said Jimmy. "It's just politics."

Benny came away reluctantly and they walked towards the fallow deer paddock.

"What was so interesting?" asked Jimmy. He'd been watching Benny's face with fascination. The dark brown eyes had never left the speaker.

"It's true what he was saying," Benny answered. "My *zaydeh* told me about it..."

"Your what?" asked Jimmy.

"His *zaydeh*," said Yaro. "His grandfather, you stupid *yok*."

Jimmy glared at him but that was all. He wanted Benny to continue. "Go on," he urged. "What's it all about?"

"Hitler's Nazis have kicked their way to power in Germany and they made Jews like us into scapegoats," said Benny.

"Why?" asked Jimmy.

"Things go wrong and you don't know how to set them right, you look for somebody to blame. That's where we come in."

"But that's Germany," said Jimmy. "What's it got to do with us?"

"Everything," said Benny. "It's happening here

38

now. My uncle Morry, he got hit over the head just walking past the Salmon and Ball."

"I've never seen any trouble," said Jimmy.

"You're not a Jew," said Yaro.

"Have you ever been beaten up?" asked Jimmy.

"No."

Benny saw Yaro's frown.

"Well, very nearly. I went back to get the tooth..."

"My tooth?" asked Jimmy as he self-consciously licked the gum where it had been. "Why, where did you leave it?"

"I dropped it," Benny lied. "Anyway, these five boys chased me. Yaro here saved me from a good kicking."

"That's what happens if you mix with the *yoks*," said Yaro. "My brother says —"

"We know what your brother says," Benny interrupted. "I don't care. I talk to whoever I want."

Watching Benny stamping away, Jimmy smiled. He looked up at Yaro and gave a low whistle. "Well, that's telling you."

Seven

"You're sure you're not coming?"

Jimmy waved Yaro away. "I told you, didn't I? I haven't got any money."

"You don't need any money. I'll pay."

Jimmy knew that must be a big thing for Yaro to say. Somewhere inside he wanted to accept, but he couldn't. His fear was around him like a cloak. He didn't want anything from anyone. He just wanted to be on his own, alone with his fear.

"Well?"

He shook his head stubbornly. "My mum says we don't take charity."

He almost choked on the words. That was the trouble; she did accept charity, and it all came from Eddie Searle. It was the talk of the tenements. She knows which side her bread's buttered, people said, taking up with a rent collector. She'll never be short of a bob or two, that's for sure.

Jimmy shrank from the words as if they were hot coals. For ten months one thing, one person had held his world together and suddenly she wasn't his any more. He had to share her with this man who smelt of beer and tobacco and linked arms with her as if they were already married.

"What about you, Benny?" asked Yaro.

"It's all right, Yaro. I'll wait here with Jimmy."

"Sure?"

"I'm sure."

"Suit yourself then," sighed Yaro, pushing off.

Jimmy dug his hands in his pockets and kicked at

40

the grass. What did Benny want? Why couldn't he just go?

"Is something wrong?" asked Benny.

Jimmy sat down and hugged his stomach as if trying to stifle a nagging pain. "I'm fine."

"Are you always this moody?"

"Who's in a mood?" Jimmy resented the questions. Who did Benny think he was? What right had he to press him?

Benny lay back with his hands clasped behind his head, staring up at the elms and beeches. "I wish it could always be like this," he said.

Jimmy was hardly listening. In his mind's eye he could see Eddie Searle sitting on the arm of his mother's chair, leaning a hand on her shoulder and smiling down at her.

"Don't you?"

Jimmy realised with a start that he'd been asked a question.

"Come again?"

"I said I wished it could always be like this," Benny repeated.

"How do you mean?"

"Everything," said Benny. "The trees, the grass, the flower beds, the animals, the lake — just everything. I mean, what is there where we live?"

"Not much," Jimmy agreed. "Do you live in the tenements too?"

"No, we've got a house. It's owned by the London Hospital."

"I wish I had a house."

"I wish I had a garden."

Jimmy grinned then upped the stakes. All of a sudden his fear was gone. "I wish I had a house and a garden and its own park."

41

"I wish I had a house and a garden and its own park and ... and a zoo."

"Yes," said Jimmy wistfully. "I wish."

"My dad says there's only one way to make your wish come true."

"And what's that, magic?"

"You've got to work hard at school; get an education."

Jimmy stared at Benny as if he were from another planet. He thought of his name written in the punishment book:

Fighting — 6 strokes.
Disobedience — 4 strokes.
Talking in class — 2 strokes.

He thought of the canes pickling in brine. He thought of every hated minute stuck in Standard Seven, waiting for the day he would escape the grim three-storeyed building for good.

"You like school?" he asked.

"It isn't a matter of like or dislike," said Benny. "It's something you've got to do."

"It isn't something *I've* got to do," said Jimmy "Where do you go anyway?"

Benny told him.

"You go to grammar school?"

"I passed the scholarship. Just me and one other boy."

"How did you do it?"

"I worked."

Jimmy's face was a picture of puzzlement.

"You remember how I beat you?" Benny asked.

"What's that got to do with anything?"

"I'll tell you," said Benny. "Was I bigger than you?"

"No."

"Stronger?"

Jimmy considered the small, dark-haired boy. "No."

"Did I have more experience in the ring than you?"

"Of course not."

"So why did I win?"

Jimmy frowned. "I don't know. Why?"

"Because I wanted it more, that's why. Winning was what mattered. More than the pain, more than anything."

"But what's it all for?"

Benny searched for a way to explain. "We get visitors sometimes down at the boys' club. Mr Jacobs invites them. 'Boys,' he says." Benny mimicked Mr Jacobs' voice. "Boys, this is Mr So-and-so, a man who's made something of himself."

"Such as?"

"Well," Benny answered, "one was at Oxford University, another had his own business. You should have seen the way they dressed! They're not short of *gelt*."

"What?"

"Gelt, shekels, mazuma."

Jimmy continued to look blank.

"Money, you *meshuggener*!"

"Why don't you talk proper English?"

"I should talk proper English!"

"Well, I don't talk foreign."

"It's Yiddish, the way they speak in the *haim*."

Jimmy raised his eyes heavenward. He had a feeling Benny was doing this on purpose, trying to tell him how much he didn't know.

"The *haim*, the old country."

"And where's that?"

"Russia, Poland, Lithuania."

"Is that where you're from?"

"No, I was born in Whitechapel but my *zaydeh* came from Russia."

"So what did he come here for?"

"Don't you know anything? It was the Cossacks."

Jimmy tried to picture a Cossack, but all he could bring to mind was a headteacher wielding a cane.

"They would ride into the village, burning the houses and beating people. You're a Jew in Russia and you're a mule for anybody to kick at. My *zaydeh* decided he wasn't staying around to get his backside kicked or his skull cracked, so he set out for America."

Jimmy laughed. "He didn't get very far, did he?"

"He ran out of money so he stayed a while working to pay the family's passage."

"So how long's he been here?"

"Thirty years."

"Thirty?"

"What's a poor tailor to do? Some of the year you work, some of the year you don't."

Jimmy looked at the sparkling waters of the boating lake where Yaro was manoeuvring the rowing boat. "Do you think your grandad will ever get to America?"

Benny laughed and held up his palm. "The hair would grow on this side of my hand first."

Jimmy gave him a curious stare, then joined in the laughter. After a few moments he grew serious again. "You were right what you said before, you know."

"Which bit?"

"About the park. This is the way things should be. There's nowhere to be on your own, no special place."

44

"I know a place," said Benny. "I'm going to trust you with this because I know we can be friends. Do you feel that?"

Jimmy nodded. "What place?" he asked. He couldn't imagine anywhere in the East End where you could be by yourself. Everywhere was so crowded. It was as if every inch of space was crammed with people.

"There's a warehouse," Benny explained. "It was owned by one of the breweries. It fell empty a few weeks ago. Here I'll draw you a map."

Benny pulled out a scrap of paper and a stub of pencil. As he drew he explained its whereabouts to Jimmy.

"It's perfect," said Benny. "It's right on the border. Neither of us has to cross out of our own territory. If you ever want me, just leave a message there. I'll find it."

Jimmy was taken with the idea. Ever since Eddie Searle came on the scene nothing had been his. The streets had been taken from him now that every boy and girl taunted him about the rent collector's visits. His home was no longer his either since Eddie Searle turned up almost daily.

Even his mother he had to share. But this! He looked excitedly at the little map. Something that would really be his.

"And nobody else knows about it?" asked Jimmy.

The idea thrilled him to his heart. For so long he had been alone. Now suddenly there was Benny. After months of distrusting people, keeping them at arms' length, lashing out when they came too close, he wanted this comradeship. He needed it — desperately.

"Only three of us know about it," said Benny. "Me, you and Yaro."

Jimmy wrinkled his nose. "Yaro, eh?"

"Don't say it like that," said Benny. "That's the whole idea of our secret place. When there are more of us, it could be the headquarters of our society. As members we will all have to stick up for each other and tell each other the truth."

"And it doesn't matter if you're a *yok*?"

Benny threw his arms wide. "It doesn't matter if you're from Outer Mongolia."

"It sounds a big thing for the three of us to do," Jimmy observed.

"So we start small," said Benny. "The thing is, you get nothing if you don't try. Like my *zaydeh* says, most of the time people think they're not even worth a farthing. Then something happens and you find out there's a giant inside them, then they're made of solid gold."

"But how do we do it?"

"We believe in each other, and from the very start everybody has to stick by the rules."

"And Yaro likes the idea?"

Benny grinned. "I haven't told him what the warehouse is for yet, but I will. It isn't much yet, just a beginning."

"What do we call it?" asked Jimmy.

"The brotherhood. The brotherhood of the secret place. Agreed?"

"Agreed."

Eight

The brotherhood of the secret place. In the week since their day at the park Jimmy had thought of little else.

For the first time in his life he began to realise that words possessed a magic of their own. His family had always been people without words, his father a shy, quiet man. Too quiet! Too easy going! How else had he ended up on the workshop roof on a sleety Boxing Day morning? It was even more true of his mother. When she was with Searle it always seemed to be him that did the talking. She just smiled and nodded. How could Jimmy be anything but quiet? But Benny had given him words — the brotherhood of the secret place.

The brotherhood of the secret place. Jimmy had something to smile about all right. The little map was burning a hole in his pocket next morning. He was dying to tell somebody about it, but there was nobody that special. He'd been a bit of a lone wolf even before his father's death, but since then he'd retreated into himself even more. Besides, even if there were some close friend, it would be a betrayal. He'd given his word.

Jimmy was walking, lost in thought, pacing his home streets before he wandered back to the flat and the possibility of another evening listening to his mother and Eddie Searle. That was when he heard it: the thump, thump, thump of a drum a few streets away.

"What's that?" he wondered aloud.

It sounded as if it were coming from somewhere

up Bethnal Green Road.

"Where's the band, mister?" Jimmy asked a man outside a pub.

"Going to look at the Blackshirts, are you, son?" asked the man.

"Is that what it is?" asked Jimmy.

"That's right, Mosley's having a parade. There'll be a fair old crowd. Not my cup of tea, personally. I'd keep well clear if I were you."

But Jimmy was already hurrying down the road. Mosley! Benny had told him about Mosley. Britain's Hitler, he called him. A rabble-rouser who wanted to blame the Jews for everything. Jimmy had to see. What was it about this man and his followers that made Benny's eyes flash with anger?

"Is the march up here?" he asked a woman scrubbing her step.

"That way," she said, gesturing with her brush. "You'd think they'd have something better to do."

Leaving her to her grousing, Jimmy ran down the street. There they were at last — Mosley's Blackshirts.

A van led the way, flying the Union Jack. Behind it, in regular rows, marched men in uniform, their faces set in stern determination. Some of them bore flags snapping in the wind. There was the Union Jack and another one, black slashed with yellow.

Jimmy watched as the black-shirted men and women passed by followed by several hundred people who, unlike the front ranks, were not in uniform. Jimmy watched, excited yet afraid, as the dense column filed into a square.

"There he is," said a man with wiry, grey hair. "Good old Mosley." Raising his voice he shouted, "Britain for the British."

The shout was taken up by a few other people but most of the crowd just looked on curiously.

Jimmy strained for a glimpse of Mosley. As he finally scaled a wall to get a better view, he heard a commotion to his left. It was the speaker he'd heard at Victoria Park the Sunday before.

The speaker-turned-heckler was yelling for all he was worth, "Jew-baiter! A lousy Jew-baiter, that's all you are, Mosley!" He was being jostled and told to shut up, but he carried on regardless. "First it was Italy, then Germany, now it's Spain. These fascists will have you by the throat if you don't stop them now!"

His protest was drowned by shouts of: "Get back to Russia!" and "Red trouble-maker."

Behind the rows of Blackshirts there was movement. Mosley was completing his march to the front.

"It's the Leader," whispered a woman excitedly.

No sooner were the words out of her mouth than a great shout went up. "M-O-S-L-E-Y! We want Mosley."

Emerging from a forest of outstretched arms was a tall, striking man in uniform. A spotlight picked him out. Jimmy took in every detail as he mounted the stage to speak. He was wearing a high-collared black shirt, a leather waistbelt, and shiny black riding boots and, unlike the majority of the men in the audience, he went hatless.

Mosley had begun his address. He was waving his arms and leaning forward to emphasise a point. "How many Jews were with Clive of India?" he roared.

"None," his supporters shouted back.

"How many Jews were with Wolfe in Canada?"

"None."

There was a ripple of applause.

"I've had enough," said Jimmy loudly. He had to say it. He owed it to Benny, he owed it to the brotherhood. In the event, nobody took any notice.

As Jimmy pushed his way through the crowd he saw a column of uniformed men on the move. A small group of Blackshirts had detached themselves from the main assembly and were breaking into a run.

Jimmy's heart was pounding. He suddenly saw their quarry. They were pursuing the soap-box speaker from the park. He was fleeing, ashen-faced and breathing heavily. That's when Jimmy saw the face of the leading Blackshirt. It was Eddie Searle.

"Get him!" yelled Searle, oblivious to Jimmy. "Don't let him get away."

They cornered the heckler in an alleyway.

"Go on, then," said Searle. "Say it again. Just you repeat what you said about the Leader."

The man in the blue serge suit was cowering, his pinched face betraying his utter terror at the sight of the advancing Blackshirts.

"Say it."

Searle bent forward and twisted the man's tie.

"Come on, Eddie," said a second Blackshirt. "Let's give him what he deserves."

"I want him to apologise for what he said," insisted Searle.

In a last gesture of defiance the heckler spat at his tormentor. Wiping the spittle from his shirt, Searle punched him hard in the face. The blow was a signal for the attack.

Jimmy flinched at the punch. Fighting had become a way of life to him, but one to one, man against man.

This was no fair fight; it was cowardly.

"Stop it!"

He ran forward and stopped just a few feet from the group. "Stop it!"

"Clear off, son," said one of the Blackshirts. "We're going to teach him some respect for a great Englishman."

Jimmy smelt the sourness of the man's sweat. He stood for a few moments, fists clenched but helpless against five grown men. The fear was rising now. It filled his mouth and nostrils, choking him. Searle hadn't even looked up, never mind recognised him.

"Please stop."

The Blackshirts were oblivious. The beating went on and on, kicks and punches rocking the curled, silent victim until he lay crumpled in the gutter. Searle gave him a last kick in the ribs then led his men back to the meeting in the square.

"Are you all right, mister?" asked Jimmy, leaning over the beaten man. There was a low moan. "Can I do anything to help?"

The heckler eased himself up painfully on to one elbow. His eyes were almost closed and he squinted grotesquely, trying to focus on Jimmy's face. Through swollen lips he forced a few defiant words. "You're a good boy to help, but there's nothing you can do for me now. I'll mend. Just talk to anybody who'll listen to you. Tell them what these thugs are doing. Will you do that for me?"

"Yes," said Jimmy, his eyes blurred with tears. "Of course I will."

Jimmy did his best to help the man up, but in the end it took a couple of passers-by to get him to his feet.

"Tell everybody," the man cried down the half-deserted street. "Tell them what Mosley's thugs did to me."

The tears were cold on Jimmy's cheeks. He stared at the dispersing crowd and he knew who he must tell.

"It's Mum," he murmured. "I've got to warn her."

Nine

"What did you have to tell him for?" asked Yaro.

"I told him because I wanted to," Benny answered.

Yaro's face was troubled under the yellow gaslight. "You must have been ashamed. It's taken you a week to own up."

"I'm not ashamed," snapped Benny. "I knew you'd be stupid about it."

"You didn't even tell the boys from the club, and they're —"

"Good *Yiddishe* boys? Yes I know." Benny was mocking and sarcastic and Yaro looked hurt.

They walked in silence down the broad pavement of Whitechapel Road and turned into the narrower streets of their own neighbourhood. Their families were waiting for them.

"There you are at last," said Mrs Yaroslavsky. "Such things you hear!"

"We can take care of ourselves," said Yaro.

"Will you listen to the boy?" she said. "And there's Mr Stoller lying in his front room with a broken head."

"Who's Mr Stoller?" asked Benny.

"Stoller, Stoller — you know him," said Benny's mother, drawing a chair along the pavement from her own front door.

"I don't —"

"You remember him," said his sister Sophie. "He worked with your father at Silverstein's."

"He got hurt?"

Benny's mother shook her head. "He got a brick

through his window, that's what he got. That's what comes of living up there."

Benny didn't need to ask whereabouts *up there* was. Too far from the Jewish quarter, that's what she meant.

"His poor wife," said Mrs Yaroslavsky. "She lives behind bolted doors. Three children they have now and they can't venture out of the house."

Benny looked along the street at the lamp-posts hung with ropes, the hopscotch pitches marked out on the pavements, his mother and Yaro's talking excitedly about his sister Sophie and her approaching wedding day.

"Do you think they'll come here?" asked Benny.

"Who?" his mother asked, turning towards him.

"The Blackshirts."

"Let them try," said Yaro. "Just let them try."

"That's my Samuel," laughed his mother. "A heart like a lion."

Yaro lowered his eyes. As the women's conversation turned to other matters, he whispered to Benny, "Didn't I tell you? You stay with your own people. Do you hear what I say? Mr Stoller tried to live among the *goyim* and look what it did for him! My brother says —"

"Your brother, always your brother."

Yaro wasn't to be put off by Benny's interruption. "You should listen to somebody for a change. Don't you remember how I saved you?"

"What's this I hear?" Benny's mother complained. "You're supposed to be friends. What's all the *schlemozzel*?"

"Ask Benny," Yaro said bitterly, marching into his house.

"All right," said Mrs Silver. "I'm asking."

"Do you think it's wrong to talk to a *goy*?"

"No, of course not."

"I met this boy, the one I beat."

"So you met at your boxing match."

"I've met him since. Last Sunday, at the park."

"And for that you argue with Yaro?"

"I told Jimmy a secret."

"Jimmy?" said Mrs Silver. That's the name of your friend?" Benny nodded. "What is this secret?"

"But Mum," Benny protested, "you can't ask. If I tell, it isn't a secret any more."

She nodded. "You're right of course." Mrs Silver was smiling. "You must go and talk to Yaro. He's a good friend to you."

"He's stubborn."

"And you're not?"

It was Benny's turn to smile. "I'll give him a chance to cool down first."

"Make sure it's not too long."

Benny nodded, then moved closer to his mother. "All this talk about fascists — are things that bad?"

"You shouldn't bother your head about such things."

But his head *was* bothered with such things. Why was it that there were streets where you played and others you never crossed alone? Why had there been Cossacks and why were there Blackshirts now? Why did his East End reek of onion and garlic sausage and ring with the accents of other lands? So many questions, so few answers.

"But is it bad?"

"They are bullies, your Mosley fascists. Old men they beat, children too."

"But will they come here?"

"They would not dare. Here we are too many."

Benny thought for a moment. "They came in the *haim*."

"Who's been filling your head with such things?"

"Zaydeh told me. He said they came on horseback and they burned everything."

"Well, so they did. But we ran once. We will not run again." Benny looked up, interested "You know what your father says about the union? You remember the story?"

Benny smiled "Yes, I remember."

"Then tell me."

"You take a match. One match you can break. Two matches that's stronger. A whole box of matches..." He made a gesture as if trying to break a bundle of matches, "...a whole box of matches, that's a union."

"Then you know why they will never march through our streets, Benjamin." She nodded in the direction of the neighbours. "You think they would stand by while Mr Mosley marches in front of their doors? You think the Yaroslavskys and the Cohens will just hide under the bed? Let me tell you the story another way." She held up her hand, the fingers spread. "One finger you can break. Two fingers together, it's harder. Now Benjamin make a fist."

Benny clenched his fist. She took his hand and tried to prise the fingers apart. Instinctively the boy resisted.

"There Benjamin, you are strong."

Strong, thought Benny, if only I were. He wanted to believe it. How he wanted to believe it! But the black-shirted men were still out there, prowling, hating. He remembered when he wasn't a fist, just a fragile finger to be snapped by a gang of *yoks*. The menace was growing, and like a mist of evil it was coming even closer.

Shaking off his doubts, Benny hugged his mother and she folded him in her arms, like he was still the little boy who clung to her skirts when strangers talked to him. He felt her warmth and her love and he believed her. He trusted his family. He trusted his neighbours. Then he turned his thoughts to Jimmy and he felt a fierce pride in their short friendship. He didn't care what Yaro said about the *goyim* — he trusted their brotherhood.

Ten

Jimmy was met at the door by his mother.

"Where have you been?" she cried. "I've been worried sick. Mrs Evans has walked around the area three times for me."

"I saw him," Jimmy panted breathlessly. "There were others too. They just kept on. They were hitting and hitting. It was terrible!"

"Him? *Who* did you see?"

"Mr Searle."

"Eddie? Where?"

"He was on the parade."

"You're not making much sense Jimmy."

"He was marching with Mosley."

"Eddie was?" She leaned a palm against the wall. "And what's this about a fight?"

"It wasn't a fight," Jimmy told her. "It was five on to one. Searle was in charge. They got this man. All he was doing was arguing back. They got him and they hit him and kicked him even when he was lying on the ground."

"Eddie did that? Are you sure it was him?"

Jimmy's eyes flashed. "Of course it was him! He was the worst."

"Come inside," said his mother, "and lower your voice. The neighbours will hear you."

"I want them to hear," Jimmy cried "That's what the man said."

"What man's this?"

"The man they beat. He said I had to tell everybody I knew what they'd done."

"Well," his mother hissed angrily, glancing down

the landing, "you're not shouting it from my front door."

Jimmy was bewildered. All the way home with every footfall, with every panted breath he had imagined her gratitude, her relief to have found out the truth about this chap of hers. His heart had sung with hope. It would be like it had always been.

"Are you coming in or are you going to stand out there defying me?"

Jimmy stared at her in disbelief. "But I'm telling the truth."

"Get indoors and no more arguing." Her voice changed suddenly. "Oh, hello."

"He's back then?" It was Mrs Evans. "I've been looking for you, you young scamp. Don't you know your mother's been pulling her hair out because of you?"

Jimmy hesitated. The man said he should tell everybody. Did that mean Mrs Evans too?

"You should give him a clip round the ear, Grace, and pack him off to bed. That's what I did with my boys."

Jimmy's mother smiled thinly. "I'm just glad to have him back."

"I'll see you in the morning," said Mrs Evans, walking to her door.

"Yes, thank you for your trouble," said Jimmy's mother. As she turned to Jimmy her voice changed. "As for you, you can get off to bed. You know what time you should be in."

"But what about the man?" Jimmy cried, not moving. "What about Mr Searle and what he did?"

"I know what you're up to, Jimmy," his mother said wearily. "I know what you think of Eddie. Well, you're not telling me who I can and can't see. If I

59

want to see a gentleman friend then that's exactly what I'll do. I don't know who's been filling your head full of nonsense about Mosley, but I won't hear another word. Eddie's been good to me, and you. Remember that flying boat he brought you?"

Of course he remembered it. It was made out of meccano and it had cost more than his last birthday and Christmas presents put together.

"But I *did* see him. He frightened me."

His mother dismissed him with an angry glare.

For almost an hour Jimmy sat facing the door until he heard the familiar footsteps. He braced himself, expecting to see the black-shirted fighter from the alleyway.

"Having words with the young whipper-snapper, are you Grace?" asked Searle, his figure framed by the light of a fishtail gas jet on the landing.

Jimmy gasped. Instead of the black shirt, Searle was wearing a fawn V-necked pullover over his shirt and tie. His flannel trousers had a sharp crease. He looked like somebody ready for a night on the town.

"You've changed," said Jimmy. "You must have done."

"And how do you know that?"

"I saw you."

Searle raised an eyebrow. "And where was that?"

Jimmy drew on his courage. "I saw you hitting that man."

"Jimmy!" His mother dug her fingers into his arm and pulled him back roughly.

"I did see him, I did!"

"And what do you think you saw?" Searle was cool, an amused smile playing on his lips.

"I saw five of you beating one man."

Searle's eyes narrowed and the smile vanished.

"You saw us escorting a troublemaker away from the meeting."

"So you were there?" said Jimmy's mother.

"I had that honour, yes."

"I've got to ask you this, Eddie," said Mrs Priest. "Did you hit this man?"

"It was the other way round," said Searle, perching on the edge of the table. "There was this rabble-rouser. He wouldn't let people hear what Mr Mosley had to say. When we tried to lead him away he started lashing out. We just took him to the edge of the crowd and told him to be a good boy and go home."

"You can't believe him, Mum," said Jimmy. "You can't."

"Go to bed, Jimmy."

"Oh, there's no need to pack him off to bed yet," said Searle. "I've got a surprise."

Jimmy's mother looked distracted. "Sorry, what did you say?"

"A surprise. For you and the boy." He must have expected her to question him further because he paused. When Jimmy's mother simply looked at him, he continued, "I thought we could go to Southend next weekend. Fenchurch Street station bright and early and we'll have a day out at the seaside. What do you think of that?"

Jimmy watched in an agony of suspense as his mother listened to the plan.

She was flushed. Her pale features had reddened visibly as she balanced between Jimmy and Searle.

"All of us?" she asked. "Even after our Jimmy's outburst?"

"Yes," Searle answered, "the lad's got a right to his opinion."

Opinion! Jimmy felt like screaming. He hadn't allowed that heckler *his* opinion.

"Well Gracie girl, what do you think?"

"I think," she said, "we'll have a lovely day."

Eleven

It was a feast. There were bagels and almond biscuits and — Benny's special favourite — cheesecake with double cream cheese. Then there was lemon tea, the inevitable lemon tea.

"And how's the grammar school boy?"

Benny had been standing by the window, hoping he could fade into the wallpaper like a chameleon.

"Well," his father said, "go on. Tell Uncle Cyril something you've learned"

Benny frowned. His father had been drinking and there was an odd twinkle in his eyes. It was always like this when some great family event was in the offing. It was an excuse to whoop it up. Benny remembered it had been the same when his older brother Manny was *barmitzvahed*. Another year and it would be his turn. Benny looked around the room and took in all the tell-tale signs. He knew it wouldn't be long before he was sent out and the room would ring with laughter at his father's vulgar jokes.

"What do you want to know?" asked Benny. He was starting to hate this ritual. Since he passed the scholarship everyone wanted him to be a genius.

Uncle Cyril winked at Benny. "Oh, something simple. What's the world's greatest ice-cream?"

Benny laughed. "Assenheim's, of course." Imitating the street-seller's cry, he sang out: "Assenheim's, they're lovely."

"There," said his father. "A scholar and a wit."

Benny took a bourbon biscuit from a plate and retreated to a corner. He listened to the loud laughter of the relatives. The spotlight had turned back on the people of the hour, his sister Sophie and her young man.

"And how's my favourite niece?" asked Uncle Cyril. "Not long till your big day."

Benny saw Sophie blush. She'd been different lately, quieter somehow. He'd noticed it ever since the wedding announcement.

Sophie's young man Nat was hovering by her chair, smiling awkwardly at the banter of the relatives.

"Can I go outside?" Benny asked his mother as she arrived with another jug of lemonade.

"Of course you can. Is it your father's jokes?"

Benny nodded ruefully and made good his escape. There was only one possible destination. He decided to visit the secret place. Jimmy had to turn up sometime.

He made his way past Black Lion Yard. Such a place could only belong to his East End. Jewellery shops, synagogues and a dairy — what a combination! Two streets further on and he saw the slats which covered the entrance to the secret place. Benny smiled at Yaro's ingenuity in arranging them to make them appear securely nailed together.

He'd come to the secret place often during the previous week, expecting a note from Jimmy, but he had gone away disappointed. He had almost convinced himself that Yaro was right. He should stick to his own.

"Ow!" His sleeve snagged on a nail as he squeezed through the narrow opening. He inspected the damage. There was a pull in his jumper.

"Is that you, Benny?" came a voice.

From a broken window the early evening sunlight

slanted through the gloom, dust motes tumbling haphazardly in its beam. There, silhouetted in the beam, stood Jimmy.

"So you made it at last," said Benny.

"Yes, I made it."

"Why did you leave it so long?"

"I was scared."

"Scared? Of coming into the area?"

Jimmy shook his head. "You'll think I'm stupid."

"I won't. What were you scared of?"

"Of being disappointed. I needed it to be special." Jimmy was standing uncertainly in the shifting light.

"I kept checking to see if you'd come," said Benny, wondering what to answer. After a few seconds he made another attempt to draw Jimmy into conversation. He was disconcerted; almost everyone he knew could talk endlessly — and did!

Jimmy turned his head slowly, inspecting the warehouse interior. "It doesn't look much."

Benny laughed. "You want to know why it's special? Listen."

Jimmy frowned. "But I can't hear anything."

"Exactly. Where in the East End can you find such a place? It's like the heart of a cave."

"But there's nothing here."

"Nothing! Use your eyes."

A look of vexed puzzlement crossed Jimmy's troubled features.

"There." Benny pointed out the remains of a pulley system. "And here." Shoving aside some old chests he uncovered a mass of rusted chains and hooks. "And what about these?" He dragged a set of harness and bridles from a corner. "They're all inscribed. They must have been used on the dray horses."

Jimmy ran his hands slowly over the treasures. "This one's got a picture."

"It's a coat of arms," Benny told him. "It's the company's symbol."

Jimmy traced a lion's mane and a scroll which wreathed around the beast.

"Families have them too. It's a sort of badge."

"Have you got one?"

Benny laughed. "The son of a poor Jewish tailor! Such questions you ask."

Yes, such questions Jimmy asked. Life was a mystery to him, hard and impenetrable. It was like a great oak door and it seemed shut fast against him. But with Benny's arrival, there was somebody in his life who had answers. With his knowledge, Benny could break through this door and unlock the mystery.

"What if you did have one of those badges," Jimmy asked. "What would you have on it?"

Benny thought for a moment, holding up the brass harness badge. "A book... yes, definitely a book... and a sword and — oh, I don't know — an eagle!"

Jimmy smiled.

"What about you?"

"I don't know."

"Of course you do. Everybody has ideas."

Jimmy looked at the badge. "I like lions."

"Yes, and what else?"

"I'd like a message."

"Message?" It was Benny's turn to frown. "Oh, the motto."

"Can you read it?"

"No, it's in Latin. I will though. I'm going to do Latin."

Jimmy looked at the script. "I wish I knew Latin.

My teacher says I don't even know English properly."

"The *meshuggener*. I'll tell you some Latin. *Per ardua ad astra.*"

"What does that mean?"

"My Uncle Cyril told me. The RAF use it. *Through difficulty to the stars.* Good, isn't it?"

Jimmy stroked the motto on the badge. To the stars. "And this says something like that?"

"Probably. Hey, I'll show you what else makes this place special. Follow me."

Jimmy walked in Benny's footsteps through the thickening darkness. "Wait for me, Benny. I can hardly see."

"Hang on to my jacket. There are some wooden stairs here."

Jimmy allowed Benny to lead him up flights of creaking stairs. Somewhere below him he could hear the scurrying of rats. At last Benny flung open a warped, splintered door.

"There!"

"Blimey!"

They were on the warehouse roof with a view of the cramped backstreets and, like a glowing ribbon, the broad thoroughfare of Whitechapel. Yellowish lights snaked towards the City, and arching above their East End was a vast, black, almost cloudless sky. Jimmy felt dizzy. It was as if Benny had unlocked the sky and all its stars.

"I bet you've never seen anything like it," Benny said proudly.

"Never."

"I came up here last week."

"With Yaro?"

"No, not with Yaro. To dream you come alone."

Jimmy examined the sky. "How many stars do

you think there are?"

"How many fleas on a dog? Thousands, millions even. See those stars. There are stars beyond them we can't even see."

Jimmy strained to make sense of the canopy of lights. "Can you see them moving?"

"Moving? You mean twinkling?"

"No, moving. Like ... like a heart beating."

Benny glanced across at him.

"Benny, you remember that motto?"

"*Per ardua ad astra.*"

"What do you think it means?"

"What it says. Things go against you, you've got to go against them. You stand up to them. You make life do what you want it to."

"Do you think that's possible?"

"Possible, of course it's possible. I beat you, didn't I?"

Jimmy smiled grimly. "For *me*. Is it possible for me?"

Benny imitated his *zaydeh*. "My boy, life is what you make it."

"I can't make *my* life."

"What?"

"My life — it's out of my hands. It just seems to happen to me. It's like ... Did I mention the rent collector?"

"Yes, I think you talked about somebody."

"He's been calling round, seeing my mum. My dad died, you see. Last Christmas. His boss sent him up on the workshop roof to mend a leak. He fell. Killed stone dead, he was."

"I'm sorry."

"I never thought anything like that could happen. I mean, your dad's there always, isn't he?"

"I hope so."

"Mine wasn't. Well, a few weeks after it happened these people came from the Welfare. They wanted to put me in an orphanage. They said my mum couldn't cope." His voice choked off.

Instinctively, Benny reached out and squeezed his arm. "It's all right, Jim. They never took you away though, did they?"

Jimmy threw back his head, as if in pain. "That's it, Benny; that's what's wrong. My mum didn't know what to do. She didn't even try to stop them."

"So who did?"

"It was Mrs Evans. She walked in while they were there. Ran them out of the tenements, she did. Why couldn't my mum do that?"

"Maybe she was still upset over your dad."

"She isn't now. She's got her new fancy man."

"Is it serious? Do you think she'll marry this rent collector?"

Jimmy shivered. "I don't know. She nearly let the Welfare have me. She could do anything. He's taking us to Southend."

Benny saw his chance to divert Jimmy from his despondent mood. "Southend! *We* go to Southend."

"We used to go with my dad," said Jimmy. "We always had a picnic right by the pier."

Church bells rang through the cool night air. "Crikey!" exclaimed Benny. "It's getting late. I'd better go home."

"You're lucky," said Jimmy as they edged towards the stairs. "You've still got a home."

Sliding back out of the secret place, Benny rested a hand on Jimmy's shoulder. "Come again," he said, turning to go. "Soon."

He was already hurrying to the street corner

when he heard Jimmy shouting after him.

"Benny," he called. "There's something I've got to tell you. It's about the rent collector."

Benny waved his arm. "It'll have to wait," he told Jimmy. "Tell me next time."

Jimmy made a last protest, but Benny was in too much of a hurry to turn back.

Benny knew it must be quite late by the time he reached his front door, but the street was still alive with talking people, shouting children and barking dogs. As it turned out, nobody had even noticed the time. The family get-together was still in full swing.

"Where's Dad?" asked Benny as he ran the gauntlet of womenfolk around the door. "Is he drunk yet?"

"Your father, he's gambling of course. Why they love their cards so much is a mystery to me."

Benny peered inside at the swirling blue haze and immediately felt the sting of cigarette smoke in his eyes.

"Is that you, Benjamin?" called his father.

"Yes, it's me."

"So what have you been up to?"

"Walking, that's all."

"You should go and see Yaro."

"I will."

"When?"

"Soon."

"Soon, soon — everything is always soon."

Benny's mother interrupted. "The family is going to have a day out. It's your father's idea."

"When?"

"Sunday."

"Where are we going?"

"For a good old nosh-up, maybe," his father

answered, inspecting his hand. "I'm not sure yet."

"Could we afford to go on the train?" Benny asked excitedly.

"The train? Where?"

He seized the opportunity with both hands. "What about Southend?"

"Southend," said his mother. "Now that's not a bad idea."

"Good," his father said. "Southend it is."

Benny felt satisfied with his evening's work. In his mind's eye, he saw two families laying out their picnic together in the shadow of the pier. This brotherhood was like the first swell of a wave out at sea. It would soon crash with mighty power.

Remembering his trophy he went upstairs. From his drawer he took the sweet wrapper containing the tooth. Pressing it in his palm, he felt strong. He'd show Yaro, Yaro who thought you could live your whole life in the same few streets, Yaro who thought people even from Bethnal Green had two heads. He would make the brotherhood work.

Twelve

The next day Jimmy entered the flat with his head down. 'Through difficulties to the stars!' The words had rung with promise sitting beside Benny looking out over the rooftops of the East End. Now they seemed a sick mockery. Jimmy was walking fast as if very angry or very frightened.

"That you, Jimmy?" came his mother's voice. She was making the bed in her room. When there was no reply she came looking for her son.

"What's up?"

"Nothing."

"Don't come that with me. What's happened?"

"I got the cane."

"Again? What was it for this time?"

Jimmy closed his eyes. He could see the expectant eyes of rows of children as he stood on stage, listening to the drone of the head teacher. He heard again the swish of the cane, and felt its lashing impact on his hand.

"Well?"

"Tubby Morrissey wouldn't leave me alone."

"Is he bullying you?"

Jimmy shook his head.

Then what?"

"It's nothing."

"You don't get the cane for nothing."

Jimmy hunched his shoulders and turned to leave.

"Don't you walk away from me, Jimmy Priest."

Her tone of sympathy was turning to frustration. "You don't leave this room until I know what's going on."

Jimmy turned on her. "I hit Tubby, but it's your fault. It's all your fault!"

"My fault? How's it my fault?"

"Because of *him.*"

"Eddie?"

"Tubby never lets up. He's always chipping me about it."

"What does he say?"

"That you pay less rent than everybody else."

His mother's face went white. "He said that? Exactly those words?"

"No." Jimmy was subdued now, his eyes lowered.

"What then? I want it all."

"He says bad things about you; that you're ... I don't want to repeat it, Mum. I can't."

His mother was shaking with anger. "I can imagine what he said. It must be coming from that mother of his. A boy wouldn't come up with talk like that by himself. Well, I'll see what Mrs High-and-Mighty Morrissey has to say for herself." She began to march out of the door.

"No, Mum, no." Jimmy was clinging to her dress. "Please don't."

There was no holding her back. Jimmy barely recognised her. Until then she had always shied away from arguments. Suddenly there she was, ready for anything. She swept along the landing and down the staircase. She paused in front of a door and began to rap on it angrily.

Jimmy cowered in the darkened stairwell, wishing he'd been able to keep his mouth shut. He saw the door open and the look of surprise on Mrs Morrissey's face.

"What are these stories you've been spreading

behind my back?" his mother demanded. Jimmy didn't catch the reply, but he heard his mother's reaction. "Don't come the innocent with me," she shouted. "My Jimmy got the cane today because of your son, and he wouldn't be saying such things if he didn't hear them from you."

Mrs Morrissey had recovered from her initial shock and began to give as good as she got. "Don't you come shouting the odds down here. We're respectable people, and it's right what my boy was saying. It's no way to carry on."

"You should keep your nose out of my business," snapped Jimmy's mother.

"Hark at you," said Mrs Morrissey. "There's the landlord fleecing us for this," she waved a hand at their surroundings, "and what do you do? You take up with his rent collector. Haven't you got any pride in yourself?"

At this point Mrs Morrissey was joined by her husband. "What's all the shouting about?" he asked. "Oh, you is it? Leave us in peace before I set the law on to you."

"I'm not leaving," said Jimmy's mother. "Not till I get an explanation."

"You'll get off my doorstep right now," said Mr Morrissey.

Jimmy leaned his head back against the brick-work of the stairwell and gave a deep sigh. Why wouldn't she come away? He felt so ashamed.

"Hello, Jimmy," came a voice behind him. "What are you hanging round here for?"

Jimmy looked up into the face of Eddie Searle. He said nothing.

"Is your mum in?" asked Searle.

Jimmy turned towards the quarrel along the

landing.

"Hell," said Searle, recognising Mrs Priest. "What's all this?" He strode along the landing and joined Jimmy's mother. Tubby's parents looked disturbed by his presence.

"Let's go in," said Mrs Morrissey anxiously to her husband.

"Not before I know what's going on," said Searle.

"Forget it," said Jimmy's mother, her anger draining away.

Searle leaned a hand on the Morrisseys' door jamb. "Got something to say to me, have you?"

The Morrisseys shrank back.

"Because if you have," Searle continued, "there's an entry in my little book which says you're behind with your rent."

Still silence from the Morrisseys.

"Now, what about an apology for Mrs Priest?"

"I don't want any trouble," stammered Mr Morrissey. "I've heard all about you."

"Meaning?" snarled Searle.

"Everybody knows how you lot settle your quarrels. I've seen you..." His voice trailed off as the pressure of his wife's hand on his arm urged him not to say too much.

"Forget it, Eddie," said Jimmy's mother.

"Look, Grace," Searle insisted "I don't know what's been said but I can guess." He turned to the Morrisseys. "Normally I'm very sympathetic to tenants in arrears," he said, "but if you're not going to help yourselves..."

"What do you want?" asked Mr Morrissey, his courage ebbing.

"A simple apology is all I'm asking," said Searle.

"Then I'm sorry," said Mr Morrissey grudgingly.

"Not to me," said Searle. "To her."

"I'm sorry, Mrs Priest," said Mr Morrissey, resentment thickening his voice.

"Let's go, Eddie," said Jimmy's mother.

Jimmy watched them as they passed him. As he looked along the landing to where the Morrisseys were still standing, he heard Mr Morrissey murmur something under his breath. "Lousy Blackshirt."

Jimmy suddenly felt very sorry for hitting Tubby.

Thirteen

"Put your purse away, Gracie," said Searle. "this is all on me."

"Oh no, Eddie. Let me pay something. What was the fare?"

"I told you," Searle insisted, straightening his trilby by his reflection in the ticket office window, "Today is my treat."

Jimmy's mother snatched at the tickets. "Three and six! Three and six each! Then there's our Jimmy's half fare. Oh Eddie, you can't pay all that by yourself."

"I can and I will, and that's that." Searle slipped the tickets into the breast pocket of his jacket with a flourish. "Now, if you can forget money for a few minutes, let's get some goodies for the train."

While Searle and his mother queued at the kiosk, Jimmy surveyed the concourse of the small station. It was crowded with East Enders taking advantage of the Indian summer to get away. For most of them it was the last big outing before autumn began gradually to give way to winter, and how they were enjoying it. Children were skipping to and fro swinging their wooden shovels and rubber pails while their parents inspected the timetable for the umpteenth time.

"Here you go, Jimmy," said Searle.

Jimmy looked at the bag of sherbet with its liquorice pipe. It should have been a simple enough present, but he couldn't see it as anything other than a disgusting bribe.

"Well, take it Jimmy," his mother urged.

Jimmy did as he was told. He could feel the bag of sherbet. It hung heavy, a badge of shame. It had been given to him by the same hand which had closed into a fist and thudded again and again into the heckler's face, the same hand that rested so easily on his mother's shoulder. He hated himself for not flinging it back at Searle.

"Hello," said Searle, noticing the ticket barriers opening. "This looks like us."

The train he had indicated gave a long blast of steam. Jimmy watched it billowing across the concourse and fading into a fine mist above his head. He watched it breaking up and remembered the starry night less than a week ago. He had been back to the secret place twice to tell Benny about Searle, but it had always been deserted.

"Southend," shouted the ticket collector. "All aboard for Southend. Have your tickets ready please."

Jimmy watched as Searle handed over the tickets to be punched.

"Do you want to hang on to them for me, Jim?" asked Searle.

"Go on, Jimmy," his mother told him. "You be a sensible boy and keep the tickets."

With a sinking heart Jimmy took the tickets. For the whole journey his mind would prey on these two things: the tickets and the sherbet. He was being bought.

Desperate as he was to stand aloof from the attractions of Searle's treat, Jimmy couldn't help but soften as they walked from the station to the beach. With the keening of the gliding seagulls overhead and the white-flecked grey of the sea before him, his spirits began to lift.

"What do you want to do first?" his mother asked

Searle.

"I don't know," he replied. "Let's ask the boss."

"The beach," said Jimmy, hating himself for his weakness. "I want to go on the beach." Then, as an afterthought, "By the pier."

"Then the beach it is, milord."

Searle danced ahead, doffing his trilby hat and singing brightly.

Oh, I do like to be beside the seaside.
Oh, I do like to be beside the sea...

Jimmy saw the sparkle in his mother's eyes and suddenly he felt lonely again. For a few moments the beach lost its magic, but soon he was unearthing crabs and paddling, doing his best to drive the thoughts which burned inside him to the back of his mind. Part of him wanted to stalk around casting a shadow over the day, but part of him sang with joy at the bright sunlight on the rushing tide.

"See the pier," said Searle. "One and a third miles long, that is; one and a third miles."

Jimmy looked at the iron construction and nodded.

"Come on," Searle added impulsively. "Let's take a stroll along it. We're going to do everything, Gracie girl; everything."

He was a puzzle to Jimmy. If he'd been frozen-faced and boorish it would have been so easy. But he wasn't. Jimmy had to fight against himself not to smile at his jokes and laugh with him as he capered along the sands.

"Make an effort," his mother whispered as Searle waved to them to hurry up. "He's so keen for you to like him."

"Come on Grace. There's something I want to show

you and Jimmy." He led the way to a candy-striped tent.

"Oh no," his mother protested. "I'm not having my fortune read."

"Go on."

"No thank you very much," she insisted. "I'd rather face things as they come."

"Suit yourself," said Searle. "I'll have mine done."

"Satisfied?" asked Jimmy's mum when Searle finally emerged from the palmist's tent.

"Yes," said Searle. "She said I was a man with a mission. It's a load of old tosh, but fun."

Jimmy smiled in spite of himself and turned towards the gleaming sea. That's when he saw the family group setting up a windbreak on the beach. It took a few moments before he realised what had captured his attention, then he saw him — Benny.

Fourteen

"Benny!"

"I thought I'd find you."

Jimmy stole a glance at Searle and his mother. "But how?"

Benny grinned. "You told me where you'd be, remember? I did the rest. I make things happen. The brotherhood has ways."

It was Jimmy's turn to smile. The brotherhood! Three ill-matched boys. At least that's what one part of him said, the part that had been hurt and hurt until it was half dead so he could never be hurt again. But that was not all of Jimmy Priest. Like a seashell long out of the waves, he could still make the sound of the ocean.

"What are you smiling at?"

"Nothing."

"My dad suggested a day out," Benny explained. "Somewhere where we would all be together before the big day."

Jimmy frowned.

"Oh, didn't I tell you? Sophie's getting married." Benny pointed to his sister.

Jimmy examined her. She was quite tall, a full head taller than her short, slightly plump mother and her thick, black hair was bobbed. He inspected the family group, looking for her fiancé.

That him?" asked Jimmy.

"Yes, that's Nat," Benny answered.

"Benjamin," came the voice of Mr Silver, "won't you introduce us to your friend?"

Jimmy cast another anxious glance in the direction

81

of Searle.

"This is Jimmy," said Benny. "The friend I told you about."

"Ah," said Benny's mother. "The famous tooth. What did your poor mother think? Such a way for boys to behave."

Jimmy smiled self-consciously, exposing the gap in his front teeth. "Mum doesn't mind. She says you've got to be tough in the Mansions."

"These days," said Benny's father, "you must be strong everywhere."

"And where are your parents?" asked Mrs Silver.

All of a sudden Jimmy became acutely aware of Searle, not fifty yards away.

"There's only my mother," he said. "She's having a rest."

"Ask her to join us," said Sophie.

Jimmy's throat tightened. "I'd better not." He saw the Silver family looking at him. "We've got things to do."

"At least you'll eat with us," said Benny's mum. "Would you like a salt beef sandwich?"

"No," said Jimmy. "Honest. I'm not hungry."

He felt a rush of prickling heat over his neck and shoulders. How could he tell them who had brought him to Southend?

"Let's go and paddle," said Benny. Jimmy nodded.

"What's the matter with you?" asked Benny as they ran toward's the water's edge.

"Nothing."

"Nothing, is it? You couldn't wait to get away."

"It's nothing to do with your family. It's ... Benny, there's something I have to tell you."

"Then tell."

"It's something terrible."

They wandered along the beach, kicking the sandy water ahead of them.

"Well, I'm listening."

Jimmy was choking on his secret, straining to find the words.

"What can be so terrible?" asked Benny, amused by his friend's obvious discomfort.

"Benny," Jimmy murmured, seeing his mother rising to her feet and scanning the beach for him, "it's the brotherhood." He saw Searle shading his eyes against the sun. He heard his name being called.

"The brotherhood?" chuckled Benny. "What have you done, told somebody?"

"It's not that," cried Jimmy. "And it's no joke."

Searle had spotted him and was striding across the beach. "Come on, Jimmy; we're going for fish and chips."

Maybe Benny didn't know who this man was; maybe nobody did.

"You should have said where you were going," Searle continued. "Your mother got a real fright when she couldn't see you."

Benny looked with interest at the newcomer. Jimmy could almost read his mind. So this was the one.

"Jump to." Searle hadn't given Benny so much as a glance.

"I'd better go," said Jimmy falteringly.

"You can eat with us," said Benny. "There's food for you all."

For the first time Searle paid attention to him. Jimmy saw his expresssion change.

Benny began to walk towards his parents. "There's still food left, isn't there?" he shouted, unaware of the hostile eyes burning into his back.

Jimmy stared after his friend, aching to run away.

"Of course there is," said Benny's mother.

"What the devil is this?" snarled Searle.

"There's rye bread and cream cheese," said Mr Silver, walking towards Searle. "Some pickled cucumbers too. I think we still have some bagels left."

Searle was speechless. Jimmy watched him as he just stared at the Silvers. He half turned as his mother came to join him. That's when it happened. Searle glared at Benny's father. "Eat with you?" he sneered. "You can keep your food, Jewboy."

Taken aback, Mr Silver looked down at his son as if expecting an explanation.

"Eddie," said Jimmy's mother, "what's wrong?"

Nat had joined Mr Silver. "Don't I know you?" he asked.

"Know me?" Searle replied. "You should know me, *Hymie*. The name's Eddie Searle."

Both men obviously recognised the name. A scream was twisting inside Jimmy, writhing like a snake. He saw Benny's eyes and the look on his face. At first it was bewilderment, but it was quickly turning to something else. It was a terrible expression, one of hurt and accusation.

Searle was squaring up to the two men.

"For goodness' sake, Eddie," Jimmy's mother pleaded. "Come away. Don't make it any worse."

By then Mrs Silver and Sophie were also on their feet.

"Please sit down," pleaded Mrs Silver. "Both of you."

Searle gave a broad smirk as if in triumph, and walked away. Jimmy's mother took her son by the wrist and dragged him along behind. "Now see the trouble you've caused," she snapped.

For a moment Jimmy resisted then, knowing it was useless, he allowed himself to be pulled along.

"Jimmy!" came Benny's voice behind him.

Jimmy's heart twisted. He wanted to run away and never stop. He wanted to be a world away from his friend's accusing eyes. Slowly, with a hopeless resignation, he turned.

"You broke the brotherhood," yelled Benny, beside himself. "You betrayed me!"

Fifteen

"There's Nat."

Benny nodded. He had made it up with Yaro. In fact, he had eaten humble pie. He had to admit that Yaro had been right about Jimmy. There was still a coolness between them though — a distance that had never existed before. Jimmy's betrayal hadn't just broken the brotherhood, it had smashed it to pieces, but Benny found himself blaming Yaro as much as he did Jimmy. By willing the brotherhood to fail he had destroyed it. Benny had a feeling his friendship with Yaro would never be quite the same again.

"I bet he's nervous," hissed one of Benny's cousins.

Nat was nervous all right. He was fidgeting with the cuffs of his suit jacket and straightening his tie.

"Ssh!" Benny was in no mood to listen to either of them. His mind filled with the sound of the organ playing and he closed his eyes. He could still see Searle's face distorted with hatred and hear his filthy insults. But that wasn't all — he had an impression, nothing more, of Jimmy trying to warn him. Benny wondered for a moment, had he blamed his friend too readily?

"What a handsome bridegroom he makes," said one of his aunties, loudly enough for the comment to carry across the synagogue from where the women were sitting.

"And he's a hard-working boy," came another voice. "He will make Sophie a fine husband. Look, here's the *chazzen*. Sophie must be here."

Benny turned to see the cantor. The organ music

changed and Sophie appeared, walking slowly beside her father, her hand on his.

Benny listened to the wedding ceremony with a strange indifference, as if it was a distant cousin getting married, not his beloved sister. He struggled with himself. Should he try to contact Jimmy, at least give him the chance to explain? Everything seemed to pass over his head: the whispers of "Such a lovely girl", the admiring comments on Sophie's wedding frock, the reading of the wedding contract in Hebrew.

Every moment of the scene on the beach played through his mind, but slowly, like the figures cast by a light show on a wall. It was as if he was trying to reach the truth through a whirl of mirages that faded as he reached out to touch them. He was confused. It had been an easy matter for Yaro, of course. The *yok* had behaved true to form. For Benny it was a torture. The moment he resolved to see Jimmy again, he would think of Searle's hatred, and wonder how his friend could have anything to do with that evil man. As soon as he decided never to see him again, he thought of the brotherhood and the attempt at a warning.

Nat and Sophie were under the *chuppah*. Benny took in the wedding canopy, then cast his eyes around the synagogue. His family had never been very religious, but the day was important to them.

Nat stamped hard on a wine glass lying on a tray on the floor.

"Mozeltov! Mozeltov!"

The next few minutes were a dizzy blur of handshakes, kisses and smiles.

"Wasn't it beautiful?" his mother asked, pressing her lips to his cheek.

"Yes," said Benny but the truth was he felt he hadn't really been there.

"Has Uncle Cyril still not arrived?" Sophie looked disappointed.

"Don't worry," said her father. "He'll be here. Can you see him missing his favourite niece's reception? Now can you?"

Sophie smiled. Benny saw the tables set with pickled herrings and chopped liver, calves' foot jelly and other savouries. He looked hungrily at the cake and bagels. He wanted to eat, but how could he when his family seemed so worried?

"Maybe you should go down and look out for him again?" suggested his mother.

"If it makes you any happier," said his father, making for the door.

"Where did he go anyway?" Benny asked.

"For a walk," his mother answered. "Just for a little walk. He had a whisky too many this morning and he wanted to clear his head. That's your father for you, getting poor Cyril in that state."

Benny smiled. To hear his mother talk you would think his father was a real *shikker*, and not a man who took his drink occasionally and in small amounts.

Suddenly there was a commotion at the door. "Come quickly, it's Cyril."

The next Benny knew the wedding guests were crowding round the door.

"What is it?" asked Sophie. "What's happened?"

Benny's mother put her hand to her mouth, then turned and tried to hold Sophie back.

"I want to see Uncle Cyril," she cried.

Benny took a few steps forward as if sleep walking. From somewhere inside him came knowledge of what he would see. He heard the questions, like voices echoing distantly in a cave.

"Where did it happen?"

"Who could have done it?"

"Have you seen his eye?"

Then Benny saw his Uncle Cyril leaning against the wall. One of his eyes was half-closed and his lip was split. His tie was pulled askew and his jacket was torn.

"In broad daylight! Now they even attack a man in the middle of the day."

"But what happened?" Benny asked.

Yaro was the first with the story. "Blackshirts," he explained. "They jumped him. Three of them, maybe even four."

Benny stared at his uncle. He wasn't badly hurt and he was already laughing about his appearance.

"A terrible thing," said one of the guests. "Terrible."

"These thugs, they attack anybody," said another.

"Anybody, did you say? No, not just anybody. It's us Jews they attack." The words belonged to Yaro's brother and they caused a murmur of agreement from the guests.

"They are growing too bold, these Blackshirts," said Benny's father, wagging a finger at his brother's face. "Look at this, will you? Now Mosley says he is going to march right through the East End — *our* East End."

The shock of this news struck deep into Benny. The fascists, here in Whitechapel! This was the thing he had asked his mother about, the thing she said could never happen.

His mother was trying to silence her husband. "Please, there are children listening."

"Let them listen!" his father exclaimed. "What

kind of people are we if we allow them to march? Do we want to see this happening over and over again? Well, do we?"

A guest, an older man wearing thick pebble glasses, tried in vain to protest. "The rabbi says we should ignore it. Let the police deal with it."

"Ignore it?" sneered Nat. "You want us to ignore this?" He indicated the puffy features of Uncle Cyril.

Benny listened to the adults' talk. He thought of Searle and the way Jimmy had hidden the truth from him. At last he knew what he must do.

Sixteen

Jimmy trudged dejectedly through the drizzle towards the mansions. It had been his third visit to the secret place. The first two had been fruitless, but this time, at last, there had been a communication from Benny — a sheet of notepaper carefully folded to form a makeshift purse.

He reached into his pocket and unfolded the package. Inside it was the tooth he had presented to Benny. Yet again he turned the piece of paper over and over, hoping that there would be a message, any message at all, but there was none.

"It's not fair, Benny," he said aloud. "You won't even let me explain."

The drizzle was gradually turning into steady, drenching rain. Jimmy didn't care. Here he was being punished, and it was for nothing, nothing at all. It was the story of his life. Things happened to him and he did nothing to deserve them.

He looked up at the Mansions. The building was grey and forbidding in the fading light.

"You!" he growled under his breath, seeing Searle emerging from the stairwell.

Searle raised his collar against the rain and pulled down the brim of his trilby. It was then that he noticed Jimmy staring at him. "What do you think you're looking at?" he snapped, taking a swipe at him.

Jimmy was surprised, so surprised that he barely missed the blow. "What was that for?" he cried.

"As if you didn't know," said Searle. "You were always out to ruin things between me and Grace.

Well, now you've done it. I hope you're pleased with yourself."

With that, he turned and marched off. For a moment or two Jimmy watched him through the driving rain.

"I've done it," he said, then louder and with a shout of triumph, "I've done it!"

He took the stairs two at a time, racing to see his mother. When he reached the front door, the welcome wasn't the one he had expected.

"What's up, Mum?" he asked, seeing her sitting very still by the window, staring out at the grey skies.

"I've fallen out with Eddie," she said wearily.

"I know."

"How?"

"I bumped into him downstairs," said Jimmy. "He took a swing at me."

She sat up straight in her chair. "He what?"

"He tried to hit me but I got out of the way."

She shook her head, then leaned it against the back of the chair. "I bet you hate me, Jimmy."

She frightened him. He hadn't expected this tiredness, the quiet sadness in her face and in her voice.

"Of course I don't hate you, Mum."

"You're a good boy, Jimmy," she said, reaching out towards him. "Blimey, you're soaking!"

"It's raining hard."

"Raining is it? I'd hardly noticed."

"What happened?" asked Jimmy.

"I told him to get out," she said.

"Because of Sunday?"

"Mostly because of that," she told him, "and the way he spoke to the Morrisseys. I mean, I went down out of anger. I'd lost my temper and I wanted to give them what for. It wasn't the same with Eddie. He knew exactly what he was doing. He enjoyed it. That set me thinking, then when he acted the way he did at Southend ... Well, I could never have trusted him again."

"What did he say when you told him?" asked Jimmy.

"He thought I was joking at first," she answered. "He couldn't believe I was giving him the elbow."

"Do you blame me?"

"How do you mean?"

"He said it was all my fault," Jimmy explained.

"No, it wasn't your fault, son. I must admit, you got under my skin a bit at first. You were right, though. I've been a fool."

Jimmy listened to the flatness in her voice. He was disappointed she hadn't got over it right away, but throwing Searle out was a beginning. Maybe eventually they'd have their old life back.

"Mum," he said.

"Yes?"

"I wouldn't mind, you know, if you met somebody."

His mother looked at him with a mixture of amusement and sadness. "There's not much chance of that, Jimmy."

"You met Eddie."

"Yes, and what a disaster that was," she said wryly.

"But I just want you to know," said Jimmy. "If you did meet somebody, somebody nice, I wouldn't mind any more." He was surprised at his own words. Struggling to explain himself, he finally added, "It wasn't the idea of you meeting somebody I hated; it was Searle."

It sounded good, but Jimmy knew he wasn't being

honest. He would have looked at any man the way he looked at Searle. But something had changed. He had realised that the life he and his mother had couldn't stay the same forever.

His mother pulled him towards her and stroked his damp hair. "I think I've been pretty selfish too, Jimmy. I won't ever do anything to hurt you. You matter more to me than anything in the world."

Jimmy felt his mother's warmth and listened to the rain on the window pane. It had been a strange week. He had lost a friend and regained a mother.

Seventeen

Benny stared at the wall.

THE FASCISTS SHALL NOT PASS

His father had been right about the Blackshirts. The word was they were going to march right through Whitechapel. In *shul* they said you must ignore the march, but on the streets of the neighbourhood it was a different story. Every wall was whitewashed with slogans. Young men and women swarmed through the area, chalking the words of defiance on every pavement or hanging banners which called the people to action.

THEY SHALL NOT PASS

"Did you ever see such a thing?" asked Yaro.

"No," said Benny. "Never."

"There," said Yaro with a proud sweep of his enormous hands. "And they say Jews can't fight."

THEY SHALL NOT PASS

Benny nodded in the direction of the slogan. "Do you think they can? Pass, I mean."

"Only over our cracked skulls," Yaro answered.

"But what if we can't stop them?"

"We must," said Yaro. "I would rather die on these streets than let Mosley strut down Whitechapel."

Benny couldn't help but smile. How he admired Yaro's intensity! He thought only of the great day

95

ahead, not the danger, not the darkness beyond the bounds of the ghetto.

Doubt never entered Yaro's head, or if it did it must be in the dead of night when he was alone with the ceiling, the walls and the cry of the wind off the river.

"My father says they want to march along Leman Street, through Gardiner's Corner and up Commercial Road."

"Yes," said Benny. "I heard that too. My *zaydeh* says there will be thousands of police to protect them."

Benny shuddered. He thought of his Uncle Cyril with his split lip and swollen eye, then of the storm gathering over East London.

"All out against fascism!" came a loud shout behind them.

"Nat!" said Benny. "What are you doing?"

"Giving out handbills," said Nat. "So's Sophie." He shoved a leaflet into Benny's hand. "Read it," said Nat cheerfully. "It's worth a dozen lessons at that grammar school."

Benny stared at the crumpled piece of paper. There was a cartoon of a man and woman, both bearing arms.

"Will there be guns?" he gasped.

"No," said Sophie, joining them. "That's about Spain."

"Spain?"

"Yes, Spain *boychik*. They're fighting a war against fascism over there."

"But this isn't about Spain."

"There was going to be a march to support the people of Spain," Nat explained, "but Mosley changed all that when he said he wanted to march

96

through the East End. See."

The leaflet was overprinted with a new instruction:

> ### *"All out against fascism.*
> ### *Rally at Aldgate. 2pm."*

"Will we stop them?" asked Benny.

Nat laughed. "Some of us will. You're going to stay at home out of harm's way. You don't think your mother's going to let you out, do you?"

Benny blushed. It had been enough of a battle to get her to give permission to box. But this!

"But I don't want to stay at home," cried Benny. "My *zaydeh* says the whole East End will be there."

Sophie tousled his hair. "It's no place for the *kinder*," she said. "Nat's right. You must stay with Bubbeh."

"With Bubbeh?"

That's right. Mum's going to be there with Dad and Zaydeh."

Benny tried to imagine his tiny, plump mother stopping an army of Eddie Searles, but it beggared the imagination.

"Well, run along Benny," said Nat, linking arms with Sophie. "We've got more of these to give out."

Benny watched the couple turn the corner, then dug his hands in his pockets. He was angry. "I will be there," he said.

"You think you will," said Yaro.

Benny was in no mood to listen to Yaro. "I tell you I will be there. I have to."

"What do you think you can do?" scoffed Yaro.

"I will be there," Benny insisted. "I will."

Yaro laughed. "Tell that to your mother."

"Oh, leave me alone," snapped Benny, brushing past.

There was a time Yaro would have come after him, but he let Benny go. Hurrying past an old man pushing a barrow, Benny put a couple of streets between him and Yaro. So what if he was younger and smaller? Didn't he have a right to take to the streets against Mosley? It was his East End too.

"Where are you going?" called one of the Spector boys from number 36.

Benny paused for a moment then dismissed him with a wave of the hand. Just then he didn't want company. Turning the corner, he found himself facing his secret place. He felt the handbill in his hand. *All out against fascism,* it said. All out.

"All," said Benny. "*All.*"

He thought of Jimmy. All right, Jimmy Priest. If you believe in the brotherhood you will come back. If you believe...

Benny pushed between the loosened slats into the abandoned warehouse and stuffed the leaflet into the crumbling mortar.

"It's your test," he said out loud. "Your final test."

Then, sitting on the ground, he buried his head in his arms. There had been a time when he resented the adult world and hated the way grown-ups kept him at arm's length from their secrets. No longer. He had believed that their world held such treasures. At last, on this day in early October, he discovered that there were demons too and they were advancing quickly on his East End.

Rising abruptly to his feet, he dusted his clothes and squatted by the exit. Glancing back at the leaflet, shoved roughly into a crevice, he gave voice to his thoughts.

"You can't be a traitor, Jimmy. Remember the brotherhood."

Eighteen

Jimmy had seen her from pavement level: his mother standing with her back to the scullery window. Even from three doors down he knew the fall of her hair. But there was someone else. His heart gave a false beat. It couldn't be! He stared at the dim blur of the other figure, but there was no distinguishing its features. It moved away from the window, leaving Jimmy to wonder.

Moments later, a familiar voice jerked him out of his thoughts.

"Hello there, Jimmy boy."

He looked up and gave Mrs Evans a broad smile.

"Worked hard at school?" she asked.

"Are you pulling my leg, or something?" asked Jimmy.

"Pardon me for asking," said Mrs Evans.

The smile vanished from Jimmy's lips. "Were you just talking to mum?"

"No, not me Jimmy boy."

His stomach turned over. It couldn't be him. It mustn't be.

"Have you seen anybody calling on Mum?" he asked.

"Yes, I have," Mrs Evans answered. "Worse luck!"

Jimmy frowned.

"And there I was thinking what a nice young man he was. Now I find out he's one of them Blackshirts."

"Searle!"

Jimmy didn't hang around to hear any more. He arrived panting on the landing and ran to the door.

"Mum!"

There was no answer. Pushing open the door, he took a step inside, but a step was all.

"You!"

His mother had her back to him. Searle stood facing her, his fingers twisting a lock of her hair.

"No!" yelled Jimmy. "Mum, you promised."

She was turning, but he couldn't stand to see her face. He had been so happy when she told him it was over between her and Searle. But she had lied.

"Jimmy!" His mother's cry tore the air, but he was already out of the door and pounding along the landing and down the stairs. Benny had accused him of betrayal and it had been unjust. But this! Jimmy saw Searle's hand, the hand that had beaten a man's face to pulp, touching his mother's hair. The tears spilled on to his cheeks, casting a bleary film over everything.

"Jimmy. Jimmy come back. Jimmy!"

His mother was shouting his name over and over, but it only fanned the flames of his shame and his fury. He was away, racing across the concrete square and down the narrow streets, his steps guided by nothing but instinct.

"Jimmy!" The cry was in his head.

Pausing only to snatch a breath, Jimmy pressed his hands to his ears. He wanted to shut out her voice forever. His mother. His betrayer.

He heard it from streets away, the strange, tinny voice that echoed eerily in the hazy dusk.

In all his misery he was desperate for a grain of hope. Then it came to him. Soon the stars would be out. He clenched his fists. This was for him; the strange, crackling message was speaking directly to him.

He dismissed the idea just as quickly. "Stupid," he

told himself. "Stupid." But the more he heard the tinny, half-human voice, the more he had to know what it was saying. He began to run towards the strange, distorted voice, excitement mingling with shame and rage.

"All out against the Blackshirts," boomed the voice, distinct at last. "Stop Mosley fascism. They shall not pass."

Stop Mosley. Again the nightmare pictures flashed across his mind: Searle punching and kicking until his face gleamed with sweat; Searle's fingers curling through his mother's hair.

Stop Mosley. The words hammered into him. Stop Mosley and he would stop Searle.

Jimmy watched the radio car cruising slowly down the street. Two men and a woman were striding alongside, giving out handbills. A youth was standing on the vehicle's running board, holding up a placard. *Bar the road to fascism,* it read.

Spotting Jimmy staring from the pavement, the youth on the running board began to shout excitedly. "Tell your mum and dad. Everybody to Aldgate. Tell them. Tell everybody."

The woman who was giving out handbills came over to him. Jimmy looked up. She was middle-aged, wearing a mackintosh and a black beret.

"But what's it all about?" Jimmy asked.

"Mosley," she told him. "He's marching tomorrow. This has been coming for months. If we don't stop him now we could have another Hitler on our hands. That's right, Adolf rotten Hitler right here in the East End. Here you are," she concluded. "All the details are there. Leave it on the kitchen table."

Jimmy stared down at the leaflet and read the appeal! *All to Aldgate.* All. Yes, all.

102

The word ran through him like an electric shock. Stuffing the leaflet in his pocket, he ran across the road.

As he turned the corner he slowed his step. There it was, the secret place. Just the sight of the warehouse lifted his spirits. He was about to tug back the slats to gain entrance when he saw a familiar figure.

"What are you doing here?" demanded Yaro.

Jimmy produced the handbill. "It says all," he explained. "All to Aldgate."

Yaro snatched it from him. "It doesn't mean the likes of you."

Jimmy tried to take back the leaflet. "It says all," he cried.

"Benny told me about Southend," said Yaro. "You've no business at Aldgate."

"Give it back," shouted Jimmy angrily.

"Here," said Yaro, tearing the leaflet to shreds and throwing it into his face. "You can have it."

It was too much for Jimmy to bear. He flew at Yaro, fists flailing. The first blow took Yaro by surprise, making his head snap back. The second sank into his stomach, winding him. That was all Yaro was about to take, however. Shoving his assailant away, he lashed out, the great fists crashing into Jimmy's chest and shoulders.

"Now, clear off," roared Yaro.

"I'm not going," Jimmy retorted. "And you can't make me."

Yaro took the words as a challenge. He charged into the younger boy, sending him thumping into the warehouse wall. Seizing Jimmy by the upper arms he slammed him three, four times against the crumbling brickwork.

103

"Now go."

"Never!"

Jimmy threw a punch at Yaro's jaw, but it was blocked.

"You're not wanted here," yelled Yaro, bundling Jimmy to the floor.

This time Jimmy didn't even try to reply. Instead he kicked back at Yaro's shins, causing him to cry out in pain. Struggling to his feet, he threw himself at Yaro, raining punches on his face and chest. For a few moments Yaro fell back, barely able to defend himself. But the two years' age difference soon told. Yaro crashed his fist into Jimmy's face, then swung the sagging figure into the wall.

"Now will you go?"

"No."

Another jarring blow.

"I said go."

Jimmy glared at Yaro with blind hatred, then shook his head.

Yaro released him, allowing him to slide down the wall to the pavement. Then, leaning over him, he whispered in his ear: "If I see you tomorrow, I'll kill you."

Winded and hurt, Jimmy listened to Yaro's departing footsteps before rising unsteadily to his feet. The street lamps were glimmering through the evening gloom, and the first stars were visible through the reddish glow that rose from the city.

Using the wall to support him, Jimmy made his way painfully to the entrance and eased himself inside. He had been sitting gathering his breath for a few minutes before he saw a piece of paper sticking out of the masonry work. Unfolding it, he saw a printed sheet. He recognised it immediately.

It was the same handbill he had been given about Mosley's march.

"I'll be there, Benny," he said aloud. "Nothing can stop me."

Nineteen

Crunch! The sound of somebody treading on broken glass brought Jimmy scrambling to his feet. His mouth was dry and sour.

"Who's there?"

The sunlight lancing across the gloomy warehouse interior was strong, too strong for dawn.

"Me. Who did you expect?"

"Benny." Jimmy sat down heavily. The sense of relief was overwhelming.

"Blimey! What happened to your face?"

Jimmy raised a hand to his temple and grimaced. His hair was matted with dried blood.

"It doesn't matter."

"Was it that fellow of your mum's?"

"No, it was Yaro."

"Yaro!"

Jimmy nodded ruefully.

"What happened?"

"He told me I wasn't wanted. We had a fight."

"When did this happen?"

"Last night."

Benny stared in disbelief. "You mean you've been here all night?"

"Yes."

"What about your mum?"

Struggling to force out the words, Jimmy related how he had discovered Searle in the flat.

"And you ran away?"

"I didn't mean to. It's just ... Well, when I saw him standing there, touching her, I just turned crazy."

"I bet she's worried sick. The coppers might even

be out looking for you."

"The coppers?"

"What do you expect? You can't just clear off and stay out all night."

"Did you leave this?" asked Jimmy, producing the handbill from his pocket.

"Yes, it was a test. Like Hercules. A test of our brotherhood. Would you come?"

"All right, so I came. Now what happens?"

"We're going to Aldgate. People are already making their way down there."

"And your parents have allowed you out? I heard people talking last night. They said there was going to be trouble." Benny went quiet.

"They don't know, do they?" asked Jimmy, smiling. "You're in the same boat as me."

"I'm supposed to be at Bubbeh's, but I tricked her."

Jimmy chuckled.

"What's up with you?"

"Nothing," said Jimmy. "I was just thinking: we're a brotherhood all right, a brotherhood of liars."

It was Benny's turn to smile. "Come on," he said. "Let's go —"

Jimmy held him back. "I've got to explain about Searle."

"There's no need," said Benny. "You're here."

With that, Benny pushed his way out on to the street.

Glancing in both directions, he led the way towards Gardiner's Corner. The boys emerged from a narrow court and joined the crowds filling the broad pavement of Whitechapel Road.

"I've never seen so many people," gasped Jimmy.

He watched as they passed in rows, carrying banners or waving flags. Flags, mainly red, were also

107

hanging from the overlooking windows. Still more banners were strung across some of the side streets, and there was one slogan which predominated:

THEY SHALL NOT PASS!

Jimmy's heart was full. He could stop Mosley, he could stop Searle.

"Over here," whispered Benny.

"What's wrong?"

"There. That's Sophie and Nat."

"Where?"

"Manning the first-aid box. I knew that's what they were doing; I just didn't realise this was where they'd be." Benny held Jimmy back until Sophie had turned away. "Quick. Follow me."

Weaving through the thickening crowd, the boys rushed on. By the time they had negotiated fifty yards it had become almost impossible to move.

"What are you young whipper-snappers doing here?" asked a tall, bespectacled man. "This is no place for children."

"Quite right," added a young woman. "You get on home to your families. This could turn nasty."

"Come on, Jimmy," said Benny.

"We're not going, are we?" asked Jimmy, horrified.

"Of course not."

The words had barely left Benny's lips when there was a tremendous surge of people in front of them. He winced at the crush and started struggling.

"Are you all right, Benny?" asked Jimmy.

"I can hardly breathe."

Jimmy clung to his friend, tugging him on through the mass of people, elbowing the close-packed bodies with all the strength he could muster.

"Look up there," he said. "That'll do." He was

pointing to the T-shaped bar of a lamp-post. "Room for two on top," he joked, shinning up, then making space for Benny.

"Benny," Jimmy exclaimed, settling himself on his perch. "Will you look at that!"

"The police will never find a way through that lot," said Benny.

"It's like this all the way down Leman Street and Commercial Road too," a man in a shabby suit told them. "They'll have to find another route for Mosley."

"Where are the Blackshirts now?" asked Jimmy.

"Who knows?" said the man. "The important thing is they're not here."

Jimmy could just make out the police lines. They had pressed forward, trying to clear a path, but now they were moving back, easing the pressure on the crowd. There was a loud cheer.

"That'll be another tram stopped," the man explained. "One driver just took his lock and walked off the tram. Now they're all doing it."

"Look," cried Benny. They've got horses." He pointed at the fringe of the crowd where mounted police were trying to move forward, but all the time more people were joining the multitude packing Gardiner's Corner.

"I didn't know there were this many people in London," said Jimmy.

"Neither did I," said the man. "Everybody seems to be on the streets. Smashing, ain't it?"

There were shouts of "They shall not pass" as the police made another attempt to clear the crowds.

"What do you think?" asked Benny.

"I can't believe it," said Jimmy. "I bet Eddie Searle's going mad."

"I hope so," said Benny. "I hope he knows how many people are out against him and his sort."

"Look down there," said Jimmy. "I saw them when I was little. They scared me half to death."

"They're the *Chasidim*," said Benny. "Frightened of the furry hats and the black coats, were you?"

Jimmy nodded, feeling very stupid. He saw the bearded Jews standing shoulder-to-shoulder with people who'd never seen the inside of a synagogue in their lives. There were no Jews or *goyim*, only people; a street of tall people.

Loud jeering greeted a clattering sound above their heads. "Are they going to bomb us?" asked Jimmy.

The questions provoked laughter. "That's a police observation aeroplane."

The mood of the crowd was changing. Their faces were less grim and here and there the odd wag was shouting out a joke, causing laughter to ripple through the throng. Even as Benny and Jimmy watched, it seemed as if people were growing before their eyes. Their East End was a land of giants.

"We've won," said Benny. There's no way through."

"Don't speak too soon," shouted the man below them. "If they don't get them through Gardiner's, they'll try another route."

"Come on," said Jimmy, sliding down the lamp-post.

"Where are we going?" asked Benny, sliding down after him.

"Where do you think?" asked Jimmy. "To find out where the Blackshirts are marching."

As the boys pushed and shoved their way through the mass of people they could hear a new chant:

"They did not pass. They shall not pass."

"Do you think we'll see Mosley?" asked Jimmy. He really meant Searle.

"I hope not," said Benny. "If we see the fascists in this area it means they've won."

His voice was drowned by new shouts.

"They're taking them through Cable Street."

"The dockers are building barricades."

"Come on, all to Cable Street."

"Dockers!" Jimmy exclaimed. "I thought they were all Irish. What have they got to do with any of this?"

Benny gave a low chuckle. "You're asking me to think like the *goyim*? It looks like there's an easy way to find out."

They broke into a run. As they looked back the vast majority of the crowd stood their ground, packing Gardiner's Corner solid.

"Do you think there will be that many in Cable Street?" asked Jimmy.

Benny gritted his teeth. "There'd better be."

As they raced down Leman Street the shouting ahead of them was becoming deafening.

"All to Cable Street. They shall not pass."

Cable Street looked like the site of a battle. Stones, half bricks, splintered wood and broken glass littered the road.

An overturned lorry lay slewed across the road; around it were heaped mattresses, smashed furniture and builders' rubble.

"What's been happening here?" asked Jimmy.

There's been fighting," said an elderly woman.

"With the Blackshirts?"

"Blackshirts?" The woman laughed. "No, they've been waiting for the police to clear the street for them, but the dockers aren't having any. Mosley won't do his own dirty work. Look out, here they come again."

The boys turned to see men and women running towards them in full flight. "Get out of the way!" came the terrified cry.

"They've got their truncheons drawn," shouted a man with a bandaged head.

Some of the fleeing protestors had stopped and were shouting their defiance. "They shall not pass."

At last the police came into view. Milk bottles were raining from upstairs windows.

"What do you think you're doing?" shrieked the woman, grabbing one policeman's sleeve. "We don't want fascists in the East End."

From a top storey window a blonde woman called down, "You're wasting your breath, Ethel." With that she dropped a vase in the direction of the charging police. "Here," she added, throwing the flowers after it. "You may as well have these too."

The gesture caused laughter from the Cable Street defenders, but that soon changed to shouts of alarm.

"Horses!" was the cry. "They're bringing up the horses."

Jimmy spun round. A wave of mounted police was bearing down on them.

"Run!" he cried, tugging at Benny's sleeve, but his friend was standing frozen to the spot.

The nearest horse was almost on top of them, its nostrils flaring, its hooves clashing on the road. Benny turned to run but slipped and fell heavily.

"Benny!" Jimmy pleaded, but Benny did not move. As the horse bore down on them his cry turned into a scream of horror.

Twenty

There was no time to shout for help. already a second wave of mounted police was bearing down on them at full gallop. There were cries of "Cossacks!" followed by a hail of missiles. Anyone who might have come to their aid was already retreating behind the makeshift barricade further down the street.

"Benny!" cried Jimmy, helplessly tugging at his friend's pullover. A second horse was almost upon them. From his vantage point kneeling on the pavement it looked massive, completely filling his vision. He took in every detail: the drumming hooves, the steaming flanks, but most of all the great, staring eyes. Above the powerful, white-flecked neck Jimmy could see the rider's face. His mouth was open in an expression of shocked surprise at the sight of the two boys beneath him.

Suddenly Jimmy was full of purpose, a savage energy coursing through him. He could feel his heart hammering. There was no fear in him any more, just the urgent need to protect Benny. He stood, legs apart, arms outstretched in a silent appeal. Later he would wonder if the horse really would have ridden over Benny, but in that moment he had no doubt in his mind. He was all that stood between Benny and the animal. Jimmy closed his eyes for a second. He felt a rush of air. Reopening his eyes he saw the horse rear, then swing away.

"Benny," he said, "are you all right?"

"Yes, I think so. I was so scared."

"Me too."

"Oi, you two," came a gruff voice. "What do you think you're doing?"

Benny and Jimmy looked into a weather-beaten face. The man frowning at them was in his fifties, powerfully built and the proud owner of the biggest strawberry nose either boy had ever seen.

"We're trying to stop Mosley," Jimmy announced.

The man tossed back his head and roared with laughter. "You and a couple of hundred thousand others. Well, your hearts are in the right place, boys; I'll give you that."

"Hey, John," called a plump, middle-aged woman from the doorstep of one of the houses. "Get them kids out of the way."

"I'm trying Vi; I'm trying." He gave the boys a confidential wink. "That's my old lady, that is. Follow me. The police might be back any minute."

There were no protests. The pair had been shaken by the fury of the police charge.

"Where are the Blackshirts?" asked Benny.

"On their way back to Chelsea," said their guide. "We got the news a few minutes ago. Mosley's been told it isn't safe to come any further."

"Does that mean it's over?" asked Jimmy.

"More or less. I heard we arrested a couple of coppers."

"We?"

"The dockers."

"But you can't arrest the police!"

"Who can't? They'd had enough. We told them to run off home and stop protecting fascists."

"But why do *you* want to stop Mosley?" asked Benny. "You're not a Jew."

"A lot of reasons," said the docker. "Mosley's no

114

friend of working folk. Besides, we owe the Jews a debt."

"Go on."

"Forty years ago we were out for the dockers' tanner, on strike for a living wage. I was only a nipper then, but my old man told me about it. There were the Jews, fresh from Europe and dirt poor, and they collected money for us. You don't forget things like that."

"John Kelly!" bawled the woman from the doorstep. "Are you going to take those kids home or do I have to do it?"

"No wonder Mosley cleared off home," chuckled the docker. "She'd scatter Attila and all his blooming Huns, she would."

With a nod in his wife's direction, John Kelly led the boys to a railway bridge. "Cut up there," he told them. "You should be safe now."

Benny and Jimmy waved gratefully.

"What are you going to do now?" asked Benny, as they left the scene of battle.

"I don't know," said Jimmy. "I can't go home."

"Come with me," said Benny. "My mum and dad will know what to do."

As they retraced their steps towards Benny's house, they could hear people laughing, singing and re-telling the day's events.

"Did you know some of the police surrendered? That's right, gave themselves up. Morry Cohen's got a helmet for his little boy."

"We found two Blackshirts wandering round. Chased them half the way to Tower Bridge."

"There's a victory march to Victoria Park. You going?"

"No, I'm off home to the wife. She thinks I only

nipped out for a pint of milk."

Jimmy and Benny exchanged glances and smiled.

A loud shout wiped the smiles from their faces. "Jimmy!"

Jimmy started. It was his mother's voice. She was stepping off the opposite pavement, followed by Mrs Evans. In one movement, Jimmy met his mother's eyes, turned and broke into a run.

"Jimmy!"

Benny was keeping pace with him, matching him stride for stride. "What do you think you're doing?" he panted.

"I won't go back," cried Jimmy.

"You've got to." Benny seized his friend roughly by the sleeve.

Jimmy struggled ferociously. Bringing his elbows down on Benny's arms, he broke free only to find his way barred.

"You can't take me back!" Jimmy raged. "I won't go."

His mother's face was white and drawn, her eyes staring. "I ought to beat the living daylights out of you for what you've done to me!" she yelled.

Jimmy raised his hands over his head.

"Do you really think I want to hurt you?" his mother sighed.

Then words were no longer enough. Jimmy felt her arms round him and her tears spilling on to his own cheeks.

"I'm sorry, Mum." She was sobbing freely. "Mum, please. I'm sorry."

"How could you do it, Jimmy?"

"I'm sorry," he said. "I couldn't help it. When I saw you with him —"

"Eddie?"

"Oh, Mum, you *can't* go back with him."

"Is that what you thought?" she groaned. "That I'd patched it up with him?"

Jimmy stared at her questioningly.

"We were having a row when you walked in. There was a knock on the door. When I opened it, he barged in on me. He told me I couldn't break it off. I was his. He was threatening me. He said he was going to have me evicted if I tried to finish with him."

"I don't understand."

"It isn't just the Morrisseys who are behind with the rent. As long as me and Eddie were..." She hesitated for a moment. "As long as we were friends, he overlooked it, but when I told him to leave me alone he turned. He called me all sorts of filthy names. He thought he could tell me what to do. A night or two up West, a trip to Southend, and he thought he owned me."

"Aren't you scared?"

"I was," said his mother. She looked at the knots of people returning from Cable Street and Gardiner's Corner. "But if all these people can stand up to the Blackshirts, why can't I?"

Jimmy forced a smile. "But how did you find me?"

"It wasn't easy," said Mrs Evans, less ready to forgive him. "You've driven your poor mother demented, running off like that. We've been scouring the streets for you. It's a good job we knew you had a friend round here. The trouble was, we didn't know the address."

"It was awful," Jimmy's mum continued. "Everybody seemed to be out fighting Mosley. We were stopping everyone, but they looked at us as if we were mad."

117

"Then we saw you," said Mrs Evans.

"Promise you won't ever run off like that again," said Jimmy's mother. "On your dad's memory."

"I promise," said Jimmy.

"And don't you worry about Mr High-and-mighty Searle," said Mrs Evans. "My eldest girl married a docker. She'll drum up a couple of big, tough lads."

Jimmy's mother smiled. "I think I'd rather pay my rent."

"Well," said Mrs Evans, "if there's any problem, you just tell me and I'll sort something out for you."

Jimmy watched as his mother hugged Mrs Evans.

"You're so good," she told her neighbour. "And I seem to make such a mess of things."

"It'll come out right, Grace. You'll see."

Jimmy's mother dabbed her eyes with a handkerchief, then looked at Benny. "And does your mother know what you've been up to?"

Benny shook his head.

"Then I think we'd better get you home."

"Children!" exclaimed Mrs Silver. "You raise them, you give them all your love and what do they do? They break your heart, that's what they do." Almost in the same breath, she was telling Benny she loved him. Finally, she looked across at Jimmy. "Where did you sleep?" she asked.

"In an old warehouse," said Jimmy. "It's our secret place, mine and Benny's."

"And that face?"

"I fell."

"Don't tell me any more," said his mother. "Just don't say a word."

"Some more cheesecake?" asked Mrs Silver.

"No, thank you."

118

"Not even a little piece?"

Mrs Priest smiled.

"You too, Mrs Evans?"

"Go on," said Mrs Evans. "Twist my arm."

As Mrs Silver cut the cheesecake, Jimmy's mother leaned over to him. "Things will be better now," she said. "I'll make them better."

"No more Eddie Searle?"

"No."

"Lemon tea?" asked Mrs Silver.

"No, thank you," said Mrs Evans. "I like milk in my Rosie Lee."

"Half a cup, please," said Jimmy's mother.

"Can we go outside?" asked Benny.

Mrs Silver raised her eyes to the ceiling. "Would you listen to the boy. He goes fighting the Blackshirts, he half kills his poor mother with worry, and he wants to go again."

"Only in the street, to talk."

"Just outside the front door, then."

Benny smiled and he and Jimmy stepped into the street.

As Jimmy sat beside Benny on the doorstep, listening to the sounds of the neighbourhood, he was suddenly aware of something, a new feeling inside him. Then he knew. It was the fear which had stalked him so long. It had gone.

"Here," said Benny, handing Jimmy a glass.

"What is it?"

"Sarsaparilla. It's nice."

Jimmy tasted it. "Yes, it is."

As they stood on the doorstep, Yaro appeared.

"Were you there?" he asked gruffly, ignoring Jimmy entirely.

"Yes," said Benny. "*We* were there."

Yaro eyed Jimmy's face.

"Didn't think you'd stop me, did you?" asked Jimmy defiantly.

Yaro grunted and stamped into his house, slamming the door behind him.

"I don't know how you can knock round with him," said Jimmy.

"Yaro? You can take him or leave him."

"I'll leave him," said Jimmy.

"I'll take him," said Benny.

They laughed.

"Here," said Jimmy. "I've got something for you."

"What?"

Benny immediately recognised the tooth in the envelope he'd made. "Anyway," he said, accepting the trophy without comment, "let's drink a toast." He clinked glasses with Jimmy. "*Lechayim!*"

"What does that mean?" asked Jimmy.

"To life."

"I've got a better one," said Jimmy.

"Yes?"

It was Jimmy's turn to clink glasses. "To brotherhood!"

Glossary of Yiddish Words
and Phrases

bagel	a ring-shaped bread roll
Bar Mitzvah	the ceremony which marks the religious coming of age of a thirteen-year-old boy
boychik	a young boy or lad
bubbeh	grandmother
Chasidim	orthodox Jewish sect
chazzen	cantor (singer) in a Synagogue
chuppah	wedding canopy
gelt	money
goy, goyim	Gentile, non-Jew
haim	the homeland
kinder	children
kishkes	guts
lechayim!	to life!
mentsch	good person
meshuggener	crazy person
nosh-up	big meal, feast
oy!	well! wow!
schlemozzel	uproar, fuss
shikker	a drunk
shtetl	Jewish rural community in Eastern Europe
in shtook	in trouble
shul	Synagogue
volla, volla!	term of abuse
Yiddishe	Jewish
yok	Gentile, non-Jew
zaydeh	grandfather